Storylandia

The Wapshott Journal of Fiction

Issue 46

Storylandia, Issue 46, The Wapshott Journal of Fiction, ISSN 1947-5349, ISBN 978-1-942007-47-0 is published at intervals by the Wapshott Press, now a 501(c)(3) nonprofit, PO Box 31513, Los Angeles, California, 90031-0513, telephone 323-201-7147. All correspondence can be sent to The Wapshott Press, PO Box 31513, LA CA 90031-0513. Visit our website at www.WapshottPress.org to learn more. This work is copyright © 2021 by Storylandia. The Wapshott Journal of Fiction, Los Angeles, California. Copyright © 2000-2021 John O'Kane and are reprinted here with the copyright owner's permission.

Storylandia is always seeking quality original short stories, novelettes, and novellas. Please have a look at our submission guidelines at www.Storylandia.WapshottPress.org or email the editor at editor@wapshottpress.org

Donations happily accepted at www.donate.wapshottpress.org

Cover image by Janine Autolitano, www.saatchiart.com/janinemarie

Storylandia

The Wapshott Journal of Fiction

Founded in 2009

Issue 46, Fall 2021
Series Editor Ginger Mayerson
A Venice Quintet edited by Dan Marcus

A VENICE QUINTET

Five Stories by John O'Kane

Contents

HYPERION TO EREBUS	1
DISPOSSESSION	33
THE ASSIGNMENT	77
FROM THE RUINS OF LLANO DEL RIO	125
ALTZ HOUSE	149

A VENICE QUINTET

Five Stories by John O'Kane

HYPERION TO EREBUS

The first time I heard of Venice, California, was at an art opening in Miami—South Beach to be exact. The artist was a woman named Daryl, a work of art herself. She was from Venice, or at least had lived there for some time, and migrated to the tropics only recently for romantic reasons, a big mistake as it turned out. The very mention of this city seemed to titillate her senses and since the gathering was pretty sparse and subdued, she took to the stage. The opening was transformed into a one-woman show. Her gyrations and gesticulations put us into a virtual trance, drawing droves of witnesses from the sultry streets. Unfortunately, she suddenly seemed to get swallowed up in the scene and disappeared.

Some months later I set out on one of my cross-country jaunts, this time to stay with friends in San Francisco and get back to writing. I took the southern route since I wanted to see the California coast. As I crept along the 405 freeway in rush-hour traffic I saw the exit for Venice, the perfect escape route for a weary traveler even if Daryl's titillations had never touched me. When I got there I cruised the area along the beach for a while and finally found a parking spot on Rose where I slumbered through a series of nocturnal noises.

I awoke to light streaming through my rear window and exited to brisk cross breezes. Trolling along a strand mostly devoid of bodies, I stumbled on what seemed like a café just opening for business. This unassuming patchwork of odd chairs and tables had no name on the front. Once inside I discovered one chalked up on the wall: South Beach Café. Was this some kind of providential pun? But judging by my subsequent chat with employees, it had nothing whatsoever to do with Miami.

  I soaked up the solars and solar plexuses for a few days, surviving just fine in my vehicle, thinking I might see Daryl gyrating in the ambiance. Once I was convinced I saw her cross the boardwalk and take flight, parsing through the crowd into the inland alleyways, but I lost her. Since she would have no reason to run from me, I assumed it wasn't her anyway, though maybe disappearing was her thing.

  I wanted to grasp the mystery of this place—what had captivated Daryl—so I asked around to see if anyone knew her, describing her performance in Miami. Many said that was a common behavior here, and one person seemed to recall her. I finally tracked her to a small, vacant church on Venice Way. According to a neighbor it had been occupied by an artists' collective but they had split a few weeks earlier and she didn't know where they went.

  By this time I was becoming quite comfortable and getting the feel of the place. I kept hangin' at the South Beach and met a woman there who had to go back east for a few months and she agreed to sublet her pad on nearby Ozone. I figured that's about how long my money would last before I would have to head up north. But as time rolled on there seemed to be something in the air, a kind of sweetness, an aura that made me want to languish on the beach and absorb the elements, lay back, and muse about purposeless sensations. As time passed I realized I wasn't alone. Many of the people I met were in transit to somewhere else and unable to leave. This quality seemed to bond us like members of some tribal family.

Though never an obsessive workaholic, my drive to finish projects started to wane, most of my time consumed with everyday life. The time flew by and my subleaser appeared, leaving me padless. My money was running low but I couldn't entertain the idea of splitting to head up north quite yet so I slept on the beach for a while and began to pen sketches of faces flitting through the breezes, spending hours and hours trying to capture the spirit of those who gravitated to this place, mostly tourists whom I never seemed to see twice.

One day—it was toward the end of June as I recall, early afternoon on a Friday—I was nursing an "expresso" at the South Beach and waiting for the low clouds to lift along with other worshippers of radiance, a scene witnessed so many times, the drooping expressions periodically transforming into anticipatory glances at the smudged, billowy gray matte above. It was always a magical moment and the longer it stretched out the better, like sex. Patches of the humid overhang would flicker like a flashlight from the heavens as if trying to fix on an elusive target and then vaporize unevenly, revealing streams of sunshine.

But on this day the divine power source barely exposed the patches and the anticipation flagged early, spiraling down into frustration and even depression. The faithful fumbled through the day, staring upward like they'd witnessed an alien craft descending on the beach. *Okay, there's always tomorrow in sunland*, the forlorn faces managed to say through the remains of the day. But tomorrow would only beget another stretch of frustration and another and...

The first few days were excruciating. Not only did the sun not break through, it seemed to withdraw further from us. During the day the streetlights were turned on along the boardwalk. Some of the truly indigent erected tents where they soireed to sunlamps, the shadows on the fabric presenting an eerie sight. Several small bands roamed the beach with nervous, high-powered flashlights like they were looking for evidence among the bodies and objects. Most of us settled in and gradually came to accept fate. We'd sit at tables along the boardwalk in a trance, like we were afraid of looking at each other and especially upward, wondering if the world outside Venice, rarely of much interest to us anyway, was the same. How fitting it would be if the end was coming in the very space that Jim Morrison frequented. The TV screens in the Bistro, however, seemed to be flicking the same ole stuff.

The gloom continued and after a few more weeks an odor started to become noticeable. At first it was little more than a fleeting bouquet of dubious denomination that vexed our torpid senses, but soon the breezes lifted and a suffocating stillness set in. A pungent smell followed that lingered for a few days. We first suspected it might be a smog inversion like that famous case in 1950s London, and several started to sport gas masks. But the smell got exponentially more palpable since the breezes still hadn't returned, and it wasn't the familiar smog odor. It was still difficult to identify the aroma's pedigree. At times it was like rotting vegetables that had marinated with whiffs of kerosene, and at others like smoldering trash doused with cheap cologne. The bodies on the beach began to thin out but soon others appeared, tourist-types marveling at the scene and capturing it through cell phones.

Then one day a gaggle of eyewitness models from a network parked in front of Small World Books. Apparently we had become a media event since, according to these talking heads, the areas surrounding us were bright and sunny. They left after a few hours but returned periodically over the next few weeks as the crowds got larger and more and more locals slipped away. The scene started to resemble an invasion and people became very edgy and unruly at times, perhaps because of the crush of bodies which made it very difficult for us residents to maneuver. It was a mystery.

Well-dressed, roving lookie-loos were combusting into fevered vectors in search of something and intolerant of their fellow invaders. Scuffles began to break out here and there and finally a full-scale melee where it seemed like people were going blindly at each other. This brought a train of K9 units to restore order. The cops carried these enigmatic strangers away but others soon arrived to fill the void. The scenario repeated itself with the new members, forcing the cops to return. We couldn't understand what possessed these people. Why weren't these odors driving them away?

We just hunkered down as the cops finally toted off most of the invaders. A few of us even ventured into the water, fairly confident now that the smell wasn't coming from some rotting creature migrating to shore.

Some of us were on the verge of following our invaders when one day one of the highest-hanging billows effervesced ever so slightly. It only lasted a few seconds, but we were still alert enough to witness this momentous event and it gave us hope as if we had injected a megadose of adrenaline. We started gazing up at the sky, beckoning for the flash to return. And then the smell seemed to slightly dissipate, lose its pungency, and we gorged on what seemed like occasional whiffs of sweet seaweed.

Our hyped-up body chemistries were working overtime. On the third or fourth day the effervescence came and left but then returned to stay, becoming stronger through the day until finally it seemed to combust a hole in the firmament that was now spreading, its edge erasing itself like it was on fire. Each day after that more and more of our billowy gray cover disappeared until the beach had returned to normal. At least I thought it had.

We reclaimed our surfeit of beach pleasures and coexisted with a tamer brood of familiar tourists. An aura of self-satisfied harmony seemed to descend once again on the community, so few paid much attention at first to a nearly transparent low cloud that would pass over different parts of the beach, sometimes lingering in one spot for a day or so. But everyone soon started to avoid it because it blocked the sun's rays and a mist seemed to drip from it.

One day after an especially rigorous run along the water's edge I stretched out on a mound of sand and awoke some time later staring up into a slo-mo shower of aerosol gloom that seemed to hold me in suspension. After staring stunned for a few seconds I managed to roll over and over like I was draped in flames and frantically trying to snuff them. Reaching the sunlit perimeter, I grabbed the nearest towel and proceeded to strip my body of its caked veneer. I couldn't get it all so I drenched myself at the public showers. Success, except for several pink blotches left on my skin and I spent the next several days feeling very lethargic. Eventually the cloud vanished for good, my skin and energy level returned to normal, and I thought little about it.

A few days later I meandered through the crush of bodies until I found a roost. It was a still and luminous day, the customers succumbing to its pleasures. A stream of what sounded like muffled chatter on a shortwave radio rushed in on me as I settled in. I jerked around for the source, but my pivot seemed to quash it. The following day the chatter streamed at me from the periphery as I strolled down the boardwalk. It was more distinct but just as brief.

A week later I was sprawled out on a fairly isolated stretch of sand near the South Beach and the chatter erupted again; this time it was transiting through erratic breezes so the sound was constantly changing tone and direction. It lasted longer than before and a relatively clear, female voice separated from the chatter-flux. It appeared to be coming from a woman sitting cross-legged thirty feet or so toward the water, but her lips weren't moving. I could only grasp bits and pieces of what she was saying— it seemed like she was emotionally distraught. Was I only imagining this, projecting what I felt she was thinking based on her appearance and mannerisms? The chatter ceased and I wandered off.

The next day around mid-morning, the sun effervescing with a crisp, cool stillness, I noticed other changes. A bright orange Frisbee sailed errantly through the mid-afternoon crush and angled toward me. I tried to catch it but it elevated beyond my reach like it was trying to evade me and then it flopped onto the sand. I picked it up and my hand tingled, the sensation spreading to the rest of my body. The sound of the waves, such a persistent yet presumed part of our everyday lives, became a symphony. I could pick out the nuances of rhythm and melody from the natural convergence of claps and roars. Big Daddy's chili dogs, usually a passable stopgap, released unimaginable bouquets.

    I nibbled my chili dog like it was a gourmet burrito from Hal's while I strolled past the Sidewalk Café, feeling like my feet were barely touching the surface. In the entryway to a boutique there was a square, head-high mirror where a bronzed reed wearing a transparent top adjusted a pair of lemonade sunglasses, gazing at herself from several different angles before returning them to the rack and strutting off down the boardwalk. I caught the reflection of a face in the mirror and immediately turned around to see who it was but I saw no one in range. Had the person been vampired from the scene? I turned back sharply while stepping in front of the mirror to grasp the elusive stranger's full form, verifying my presence by raising my right hand. I was the stranger!

    I pondered the visage. My eyes were like simmering, azure-blue saucers in a surrounding pool of calm, milky water. They seemed to be smiling in sync with my lips, which appeared healthier and had a curious curl, all apprehension erased like someone else's face was fleetingly superimposing on mine. Had someone given me a makeover without my consent? My posture was improved and my skin was tauter. My hair was curlier and more voluminous. As I reached up to touch it a gaggle of multi-colored sunglasses invaded my space, edging me onto the boardwalk.

    I trotted straight to a table across the way where tarot reader Musina, a casual acquaintance, was servicing a client. I circled around the table a few times and she finally glanced up at me for a split second before resuming her focus, but suddenly sprang from her chair and stepped toward me.

"What are you... what have you done to your... face, your body?" she asks, semicircling me.

"I haven't done anything," I protest.

"You must be having an... enlightened day or... you've found a new substance."

"I'm not high on anything and I feel normal... totally relaxed." She looks perplexed but her face slowly sympathizes and then erupts into a sardonic yet savory smile.

"You're into... something... chemical, mineral or... spiritual!" She glances at her client, absorbed now in our interchange, and apologizes for the delay. He strains an acceptance while glomming on me briefly, then fixes his glance on her. She's thinking of me as a client, wants me to sit down and chat, fit me to a card, but senses that my head is imploding with confusion. Then her thoughts momentarily disperse, like her mind is an analog television losing its reception. When they return, she becomes fixated on the idea of fate. She's thinking I'm probably a fool and ready to go over the edge. This thought then disperses and she stares at me soberly while a series of erotic images flood her mind. Meanwhile, her client has begun to x-ray her taut behind.

"I'm into movement," I say. "I gotta get out and explore this..."

"...you need to focus, channel that energy into something productive."

I was several feet away by the time she finished her sentence but I could still make out her thoughts as they weakened. She said she wanted to get me into a group and try out some new therapies. Before I could grasp the full gist of her reflections I was too far away and chatter began filling my head from different directions. But certain streams began to separate from the others, reasonably coherent sentences that stood apart from the noise. I looked around to identify the source of these streams and it appeared they were coming from various distances. The harder I tried to concentrate the more they clarified themselves. It was like a censoring filter had been implanted in my brain.

Wondering if I could turn it on and off, I shuffled further down the boardwalk and took refuge near a small eucalyptus with overhanging branches. It was a fairly secluded spot where I could meditate. The increasing repression of external stimuli left me in a cocoon, a time warp. The silence spoke through visions. I saw hundreds of shapes speeding through space, many of whom I recognized, all trying to connect with each other. When I came out of it after about thirty minutes, the chatter of voices resumed but I seemed to have an even greater ability to repress streams. I could blot out virtually all the noise around me. But I could also single out other streams for clarity, like I was manipulating tracks on a recorder. Would I have to recharge this power frequently through meditative sessions to avoid losing it?

With this arsenal at the ready I rejoined the boardwalk flow toward the Circle, cobbling the errant musings to test my editing savvy. They were mostly banter so I sent them to my recycle bin and took in the sights on the east side. I was drawn in by the lettering on the advertising placards, most of them feeble efforts to seduce the unsuspecting stroller. The letters started to move slightly, some turning clockwise for a split second before springing back to an upright position and then vibrating for several seconds more. Soon all the letters were shimmying and I could virtually feel their tactile qualities without touching them. Then they joined in a visual maze that piqued my interest like a complex work of art. Was it created by the same forces that gave me this power?

    I felt bodies around me and the letters dissolved into a blur of jagged lines and smudges. A crowd of people was circling me, ogling my facial expression. I sensed it might be difficult to escape but the bodies melted away as I divined a lane. Once away from them I saw three young, clean-cut males, all wearing the same tees with a logo I couldn't decipher, snapping pics with their devices like they were witnessing an important public spectacle. I shuffled further down the boardwalk and noticed that they appeared to be shifting with me. I faced them straight on and they widened their panorama so I hustled across the boardwalk and grabbed a chair at the end of a long table occupied by a group selling salvation to strolling sinners with xeroxed Bible snippets. From this vantage I could see the three males had ceased their shuttering and were gazing through the crowd, apparently looking for something or someone. I concentrated hard to hear what they were thinking but for some reason all I heard was a gurgling sound. Were my powers being interfered with? Perhaps their devices had erected an electronic shield. They began to drift apart, like they'd decided to scout in different directions, and the gurgling sound splayed, each one carrying an inflection. After a minute or so the interference had lifted and I could hear some broken phrases, but they were apparently coming from only one source. It was like the three were expressing their thoughts in unison. Or was one of them simply setting the stage, the others deferring respectfully to their collective voice? Could a single mind be mute? The phrases started to come in clearer with each passing moment.

"We can't lose... it would be... for the community. Once he... the rest... will... try and... whatever they... slope. We have... way to... him."

Finally, the first few words of a sentence peeled off, but before they could be deciphered a strong gust of wind whipped along the boardwalk corridor, dispersing the crowd. As stillness was restored a cluster of small black clouds drifted over us, striating the area in shadows and causing many to gaze up at the source. Squalls began to splat the pavement erratically, followed by a smattering of hail, sending most everyone for cover. I slipped under the nearest eucalyptus and scoped the mayhem. I thought I saw one of the young males from earlier crouched under a table in front of the adjacent café but I could only retrieve static.

As the final cloud evaporated I spurted across the sand toward the water. I could hear low-level chatter mixed with static erupting from different directions, but my vision was blurred. I couldn't see the faces of the people strung out on the sand. In fact I could only see the outlines of bodies, like they were heat-haloing, but it wasn't a hot day. I blinked and the spaces between the lines started to fill in slightly as the chatter became easier to discern. Thinking that I saw the males on the fringe of the sand scoping the area, I continued further south, angling toward the water. I weaved through the clusters of bronzed bodies, the forms becoming more distinct now. Thoughts were lofting through the air like errant Frisbees, ready to pluck, and getting clearer and clearer. At the same time I was getting looks from people, nervous double takes, like I had suddenly been conjured from the breezes or the ether. Had my appearance changed?

"You from the theater troupe over on Abbot Kinney?" spouts a fifties-something, silver-haired punkish woman, her long slender body stretched supine across a mound of sand. She could be posing for a shoot in a high-fashion mag. Her bronzed skin is strikingly smooth and taut.

"You just get otta rehearsal for a Greek... comedy, dearest?"

"You're fantasizing what will happen when you get back to your apartment, when you meet... him. He promised that when you meet today..."

"...what are you... how do you know..."

"...that's why you're so happy. But you're also worried because the last time he didn't show and..."

"...what are you, some kinda... seer? Come here and talk to me."

"I'll spoil your fantasy... your reunion."

"What'd you do to your eyes? You on something? Can I get some?"

"Where'd you get that haircut," interjects a surfboard-laden male from about twenty feet away, frozen in his tracks. "You don't look like you're from around... here." His expression would not inspire a welcoming committee.

"You're thinking I'm not of... a normal persuasion."

"What do you... who are you?" He looks at me like he's seen a ghost.

"I know you!" peals a raspy voice to my right. "My lover's come back for me!" I see a stout woman of indeterminate age hobbling through the sand with outstretched arms, finally stumbling a few feet in front of me. She looks up and screams, turning several heads nearby. She's thinking of how close she came to getting some spare change. Meanwhile, two hulking Samaritans gallop to the rescue, rearing up as I trot further down the beach.

A small group of men and women of various ages, similarly dressed, are languishing in a semicircle near the lip of the sand and playing drums. They're striking them very tentatively like they've just started rehearsing for a drum circle performance. Their sounds seem out of sync but convey a curious cadence that soothes. I step around them but no one looks up. They seem at one with their task, their thoughts expressed in flatlined sighs with an occasional hiccup. One woman finally notices me out of the corner of her eye and gives me a graceful once-over, winking a welcome. I edge between two members, ready to merge into the mass, when a wave of pain, shorn of any thought, jolts me. The intensity is so palpable that I immediately assume someone is dying. I look around and there's no one close who fits the bill so I backstep from the circle, apologizing to the woman with a wink, and troll north along the edge of the water where the greater share of bodies languish.

I walk several feet before another pain-wave pelts me, this one even stronger than the first. It seems to be coming from a woman humped over a mound of sand at the edge of a cliff, roughly ten feet above the water and about fifty feet from me. I veer right onto the soft sand and plod toward her position. As I get within about ten feet she throws her head back ferociously, staring straight up at the sky, then slowly drops it level with my sightline, remaining frozen in this position as if she's meditating though her eyes appear to be bulging. I can't cull her thoughts. All I hear are discordant gurgles clashing. She still doesn't budge. I step closer and feel horror effervescing from her body as she recoils back to a safe angle. From my angle she seems to have a smile on her face, but of a type I've never seen before. Her facial muscles seem stretched, contorted, and her mouth is wide open like she's ready to shriek. She continues to hold the same pose, I wonder for how much longer. I step closer, but not too close since I don't want to alarm her. If she drops from the edge she could die.

A gaggle of young sun worshippers flounder toward her from the other side, causing her to flinch, and her horror surges a few octaves, now lisping with a few alien phrases. I'm tempted to rush around her and chase them away.

"That's one a those hippies that keep hangin' around here, guys. Let's carry her off to the dumpster!" As he smirks to his commiserating party he imagines what it will be like to take off her top.

She pivots her head toward them ever so slightly, like she's afraid of what she might see, and meets their blanched, frozen expressions. They finally bust a gut and strut off to another attraction.

Returning to her original pose and expression as if nothing happened, she drops her head between her knees and remains motionless. She's wondering why they looked at her the way they did; why they didn't come over and talk to her in a normal way. I wonder why she would even want to talk to them, what she thinks would come from that. I wait for an answer but only feel another surge of pain from her body. Certainly not your typical beachgoer, she's wearing a long, loose-fitting, black gauzy dress, more like a nightgown, which meshes visually with her medium-length, coal-black hair. Her skin is bleached white. I shift slightly and see what seem to be marks on her arm. Apparently feeling my presence, she swivels toward me abruptly but just as abruptly turns back. She's thinking I'm a threat to her. Her eyes! Her eyeliner is so thick and black that they can barely be seen, and the ashen color of her whites helps to repel the light, hide her qualities. Did she really see me? Her thick black lips are pressed together in a pout. Is she a sorceress beamed here from another space and time, or has she wandered away from a gothic costume party?

She's thinking how refreshing it would be to walk into the cool sea and pulls her head up erect, staring off into the horizon. Her head bursts with fragments of speech and she jumps up, doddering away from me. Assuming she plans to descend to the water I follow her. As I get close she turns around sharply like she's annoyed at being followed but only stares at me blankly.

"Don't go near the water!" I blurt, dissolving her stare into a series of Morse-code blips. "It will be dangerous... you don't want to go there."

She delivers a long steady dash and looks dreamily off to the water, turning back toward me but short of full eye contact. "How did you know I... are you following me?" She now connects but only for an instant and begins backing away from me, down the slope toward the water, evading my gaze. "I need to... cleanse myself. Please let me..."

"...you won't be cleansed. You'll disappear."

"I need to be somewhere else."

She channels my gaze and seems partially blinded by what sustains this connection.

"What's in your eyes?' she asks. "They're bright,

pulsing. And your complexion, it's... glowing."

"Maybe you're not used to the light outside. It's a pretty bright day... a luminous day, the type we get only once in a while."

She's still locked into my gaze. "The light out here is too much... it suffocates. And it seems to force people into meaningless behaviors."

"The excess of brightness and the crush of bodies can empty us. It's an extraverted playground for many. But continued exposure to the light can also enlighten."

"We need gloom and... contrast to get inspired."

"Yes, to get some perspective... get into ourselves. But we can learn to find outlets for that here."

"Your... glow made me feel weak at first but now I feel warm inside like a new kind of strength is forming. Are you on... substances? You seem to be looking into and through me. Is that how you got into my thoughts?"

"No... nothing like that." I hear white noise oozing around us and a pulsing of chatter. A few clusters of spectators form nearby. "Let's head over to that tree... the shade might help you... us." In transit, I spy the boardwalk traffic and think I see the three males playing sentry in front of Small World Books.

It's refreshing to get into the shade. I was beginning to feel a little weak myself, my energy level starting to diminish as I faced off with her. The blackness weighed on me somehow. I look at her and she seems content now, staring out to sea. She's thinking how soothing the water looks but there's no inkling of any destructive urges. I guess I've halted her designs for the moment and drawn some of the pain from her. And now I feel like I'm getting stronger too.

Where is this strength coming from? What has she done to me? She flinches and her thoughts rush me. She's worried, feeling that some people are coming too close to her and they seem aggressive. I look around and see more and more clusters of people shuffling in our direction, but I'm not sure if they're concerned with us. Is she feeling something I'm missing?

A wind gust sprinkles a few grains of sand on us, but the return to calm is short-lived. A firm and persistent breeze passes through our area and by the time it ceases we're draped in shadows. I see now that even more clusters of people are milling around us, and we're certainly the focus of their attention. I hear snips of hostile chatter.

The stillness suffuses with rain squalls and she stirs, looks around, and rolls over to her right. She's thinking they're definitely coming after her but sees no escape path and remains firm, glancing at me for support. The wind becomes stronger and I see a large cloud passing overhead that seems to grow as it moves. The clusters now disperse into spectators devoting their attention to the heavens. Every few minutes there's a lull. The sun peeks through, smooching the nervous body parts and patches of abandoned sand plots, but the cessations are brief and followed by a more intense onslaught from nature. She's pondering what to do and jerks away from me but stops in her tracks, again glancing at me for support. Her expression contorts to fear. Is she reacting to my expression? It seems she's not going to flee to the ocean waves but I can't get a clear image now of what she's thinking. A few of the bodies resume their attention to us but I hear only static from them.

The sand begins to loosen around us and the bodies disperse again. I slog to a firmer patch, pulling her with me. The breezes blow stronger and at volatile cross-angles. A strip of light separates the shadows and shards of what appears to be garbage surfacing in a sand patch. Soon there's a mound of rancid refuse and we hustle toward the boardwalk. Another strip of light appears and I see white caterpillars spread over the sand in a provocative visual design. I strain my mental powers to interpret it as more rain squalls pound the area and we continue on through the scattering bodies to shelter. She follows contemplatively behind me but her expression evokes horror. I can't get an indication of what she's thinking.

We follow the throng off the sand, the severity of the wind and the now-persistent downpour having nearly turned the beach into a vacant lot. The boardwalk is dense with soaked seekers of cover. We manage to grab a couple stools alongside a burger stand on a narrow street that abuts the boardwalk, barely fitting under the awning, bodies pressing against us. Some start to fight over spaces while others, gazing hopelessly up at the drenching heavens, start to laugh uncontrollably, fomenting a party atmosphere.

Hunkered down, we swivel-stutter toward each other like we're each stealing a peek at some forbidden image. We glimpse each other and swivel-stutter slightly away like the mystery of it all produces pain, or at least a modicum of shock.

"Your face... what happened to it?" I ask, trying to read her thoughts but having no luck. Her makeup is smeared, the effect of the wetness making it appear that she has a bleeding wound. But her face is rejuvenated, like the excitement has pumped up her emotions.

"Nothing I... know of. But thanks for getting me away from the water's edge. I feel a lot better."

"You seem more relaxed and confident." I still can't grasp what she's really thinking.

"Your face, it's sunken. Your hair seems thinner. Your skin is grayish. Your eyes seem to have changed color."

"The weather I... guess. I've always been affected by it."

The wind whips to a frenzy, sending pieces of clothing and beach detritus airborne. A few frail figures fall to their knees momentarily. We hold onto our stools tightly but a bulge of frantic bodies knocks us off. We roll across the pavement to avoid being crushed by the next wave, remaining flush against a building. The intensity of the wind persists, and with it comes a soufflé of putrid odors that's saturating our space. I manage to get up and spy the surrounding scene while stepping a few feet into the gridlock. When I turn around she's gone. I try to locate a lane to search for her but the crush of bodies has apparently collapsed around her so I drift at the whim of the mass. A break in the downpour checks its momentum and produces a few convenient fissures. I slip into one of them and trudge along the boardwalk, exiting near Windward, still no glimpse of the mystery lady. The worst of the storm seems to be over. Some are returning to the sand; others make their way to the parking lots.

As I turn left on Windward a trio of phones pulses through a parade of shopping carts and hustles toward me. As they get closer I see that it's the three young males and I'm apparently in their crosshairs. A family of tourists wobbles by, screening me from the three momentarily, so I scat up Windward to Speedway and turn left, blending into the flow. I glance back and see my pursuers shooting their weapons wildly in all directions.

My car is parked on Main just down from the Christian Science Church wedged between a Hummer and a recycled school bus—neither of which has been moved for several days—beneath a large shade tree. It's been my home for a while and feels especially secure now since the only way someone could see me would be if they slip around the tree and peek in the passenger door. The rest of the windows are covered, including the windshield. A perfect condition for relaxation. The chatter comes and goes now, none of it very clear, and it's hard to figure which direction it's coming from. Perhaps a nap will help my mind work better. Now if only the weather will cooperate.

I awaken to two bulging eyes, one on top of the other in a line perpendicular to the base of the passenger window, the one on the bottom seemingly larger, the forehead slightly obscured but the oval in-between fully identifiable as a mouth despite its upright tilt. It's enough to identify Panos, a gypsy who lives with his extended family in the school bus. He pivots his head clockwise and I realize he was probably trying to get a glimpse of my angled head, not sure it was me. Great to have good neighbors! But now he twitches counterclockwise and back, giving me a straight-on gaze that seems to suggest he doesn't realize I'm me, that perhaps someone has slipped into my car for a respite. He suddenly vanishes like maybe he's afraid I'm going to chase him down for violating my space. Or maybe...

The events from earlier play back in my head like an unedited strip of film and repeat in varying sequences, inviting me to make them cohere. I try with some success. The nap has given me a clearer head but the effect doesn't last. The chatter rushes me, scrambling my efforts, and fades to blank. I recall what the mystery lady said about my appearance and the fatigue I felt and the struggle to glean what she and others around me were thinking. My car had been marooned on this spot for a while and the rearview mirror is askew. I inch it toward me, finally adjusting it firmly into position, and blink rapidly as though what appears on the glass might vanish. I've got to stop looking in mirrors. I never did trust them anyway. Will everyone now start reacting to me like Panos did? I need to get away from this area for a while. A good stroll will do me good.

A friend of Musina's I'd met at her table one afternoon a few weeks ago had a studio just beyond the Venice border and welcomed all of us to drop in when we were in the neighborhood. I had logged a little time in that area when I first arrived so her directions stuck in my mind.

I welcome the chance to get out of the car and stretch. Plus the sky is nearly cloudless and the air is pleasantly breezy. As I enter Abbot Kinney I try hard to concentrate on a woman with orange hair adorned in Day-Glo colored military fatigues and sporting a black bandana covered with white peace signs of varying sizes and designs. She begins to weave in and out of the sidewalk traffic blowing soap bubbles in the faces of the well-dressed restaurant seekers and smiling ecstatically as most cringe. Some back away from her and others berate her with threatening language. I hustle as close to her as I can but all I hear is faint, gurgled chatter and I'm not even sure she's the source. Suddenly a series of chatter-streams rush me, pushing what could be hers into the background, but these vanish just as quickly as they erupted. This more recent chatter is somewhat clearer but it lasts only for an instant and then becomes very faint—

fainter than the earlier version.

I wrack my brain trying to absorb the final flickers, my physical contortions apparently drawing the attention of the strollers.

"Call the police... get these people out of here!" screams a young woman Guccied to the hilt, reining in her oversized, barking Weimaraner. The apparent association of the woman with me sends a signal to the crowd that secures our partnership in crime and several concerned citizens see me for the first time.

"Look at his face!" screams an anonymous. "He looks evil... he must be on drugs."

As the woman blows bubbles to the heavens in the middle of the street I split up the nearest side street and saunter east through the back alleys, occasionally encountering a perplexing stare but nothing more. I more or less blend into the new surroundings. The chatter is now quite weak except for an occasional rush, but the rushes are very intense and painful. They make me feel like my head is going to explode. I zigzag through the traffic across Lincoln above California and follow Lincoln north for a block or so when I get another jolt. This time it lasts longer and I collapse onto a bus bench, clasping my head. It passes and I turn to see a crowd of people milling around a building on the corner set back a hundred feet or so from the sidewalk and adjacent to a strip-mall. It's a two-story structure that looks like it was once a retail outlet. Burglar bars cover nearly the entire front and behind them is the familiar gray sheet-metal slab that slides horizontally, likely replacing what was once a glass plate during a more secure time. Several handymen are inspecting this façade, their tools and cans of paint at the ready. There's a sign lying askew on the cement but I can't read the partially obscured letters.

"Do you need help to get inside?" asks a woman who spurts from the crowd, gesturing like an imaginary first responder. A few others trail her. The chatter has stopped but my head hasn't returned to normal. It's a hushed void, all external noises suspended. Her words come at me like stuttering splashes on a calm lake.

"Inside to... what?"

"Services," spouts one of her followers, an austere but sprightly young male. "We're getting ready for our meeting."

"Service for... what?" My head begins to fill with mild whispers.

"For our souls," interjects the woman.

They coax me into the queue, which is filing through the side door much more quickly now, but I hang back. "Is this a mission?"

"No... well, sort of," she says. "Depends on what you mean. We aren't down and out and lookin' for a handout... nothing like that. We're active participants in a mission that constantly evolves. We meet every day and..."

"...that's a lot of service." The whispers reach a crescendo and abruptly cease. I step back toward the street.

"Come and... meet our parishioners."

I let them cup my wrists and glide me into the queue. When we come within a few feet of the entrance my head explodes again and I buckle. They escort me through the door into a room that's being made over. The interior walls and the ceilings are being knocked down. Boxes are being piled along one wall. One dilapidated shelf along another wall sags with cumbersome, vintage vacuum cleaners, hoses, and myriad other unidentifiable parts. Chairs are being set out in rows in front of a stage at the far end of the room.

"You need to clear your head... you must be having bad thoughts. You're probably losing touch with the spirit and... your self. You need to find your new self and re-align with the spirit. Spirituality and identity are linked. Providence has sent you to us."

"I'm not sure I..." The pain lifts but my brain cells feel sluggish.

"You need to purify your lifestyle."

"I thought it was pretty..."

"We're the Everyday Re-Inventists. We were founded in the '70s as a spinoff of the Seventh Day Adventists. They believed that too many people were developing false selves and following false idols and the solution was to get into the scriptures and await the Second Coming of our savior while living blessed, Christian lives. We've evolved through several other spinoffs since then and were refounded a few years ago under our current name... a new name for a new era. Our one sure plank is that we must adapt to changing times. Nothing stays the same. Including our lodgings... our church. We move around a lot to different sites because the sensation of starting anew keeps us focused on the power of change. Plus we've accumulated enemies over the years and... it's not always easy to come up with the rent. We feel the Second Coming has already happened... the Lord is among us and in any one of us at any given time. Scripture is important to us. Our library is full of the important biblical texts and we absorb the ones that work for us at the moment. We believe above all in self-transformation. Come... come to our purification chamber where we can delouse you. Once we do this you'll be ready to begin living a clean, selfless, spiritual existence.

"I don't think I'm... ready for... that," I manage, pivoting away from them, my head pretty clear now. Several others in the room creep toward us, their faces more flummoxed than alarmed. I attempt a smile while fading left, assuming I will soon be surrounded and likely commandeered. But the flock merely glares with peevish rapture as I edge anxiously through the door.

My car, I've got to get to my car. I skip through the strip mall and sprint across Lincoln, barely slowing as I veer right and then left at the first street. A block or so into my jaunt my head explodes again and I stretch out on a front lawn until a woman armed with a broom flails me down the street. This time my head keeps pounding and I wander aimlessly, finding myself suddenly in an unfamiliar neighborhood. I ask an elderly woman walking her dog where I am and she blinks at me for several seconds while looking me up and down, saying, "The clinic is... two blocks over on... Rose."

A clinic is the last thing on my mind. I only want to get reoriented and find my car. If I get to Rose, though, I shouldn't have any trouble getting there. But the more I think about it, the woman might've done me a service. My head still hasn't returned to normal and maybe I can get some help.

The Free Clinic and Healing Center takes up about a half block on the south side of Rose. It looks different than the last time I passed by, when it was merely called the Free Clinic. The outside has been painted and a new sign hoisted atop a second floor add-on, reflecting what appears to be a widening of its focus.

The waiting room is nearly full and many of

the customers—mendicants of diverse persuasions probably thankful for the chance to get off the streets—are zoned out, though a few seem like they've found themselves in the wrong place and for some reason can't manage to escape.

"I want to... see someone about..."

"...Visa or Mastercard?" quips the receptionist without looking up, a thirty-something woman doodling on a newspaper.

"I thought it was... free."

She reaches for a folder and begins to peruse its contents, still no eye contact.

"I have some money if..."

"...if you don't have a card just have a seat," she mouths methodically.

A musical cockney accent with an Angeleno affectation pierces the relative calm on my right and the receptionist twitches before glancing over at the source, catching my face in nearly the same instant. She juts up from her chair, looks at me, then the accent, then at me again and quivers her mouth muscles into formation for a scream that never arrives, stalled between the idea and the execution of an emotion. I keep waiting for the sound to engulf us but she rushes down the hall, leaving us in suspense, then returns quickly with two white-coated helpers, one male and the other female. Their eyes range over me in slo-mo but their bodies pull back in fast-forward. As they contemplate their next move, the receptionist consumes the accent.

"Come with us, sir!" spouts the female while the male carefully clasps my hand and edges me toward the area they came from.

"Why? What are... where you taking me? I thought I had to... I don't have a card."

"Just follow us. We're here... to help."

We end up in a large room that looks and feels like a coffee-break space except that a desk, a shelf full of books, and a long leather sofa fill the far corner. They position me on the sofa and pull up chairs, one on each side. My head has been cool and silent for a while but I start to hear chatter again. It's very low-level and mostly static.

"Are you okay?" asks the female as I concentrate on the sounds, trying to glean the content and the source.

"Yeah, I just have a bit of a... headache."

"Let's talk about that," says the male. "You seem to be under a great deal of stress. Your face, it's... sunken."

I feel limp, like the energy is draining from my upper body. "I've been having headaches since earlier today... ever since the storm passed over."

"Storm? What storm? Here? Here in Venice?"

"Yes, down near the water. I was enjoying a beautiful day and listening to conversations... thoughts and... voices, many voices that were... and then I..."

"...tell us about these voices," says the female. "How long have you been hearing these voices?"

"For a... few weeks."

"Are you having issues with your wife, mate... family?"

"No, nothing like..."

"...have you ever been professionally evaluated?" interjects the male.

"No, I... it was a beautiful experience... I could see so many things and... I heard these people saying what..."

"...what was your relationship like with your

father... your mother?"

"It was... okay... but no, no, that has nothing to do with..." I hear someone mumbling something. It becomes clearer and clearer but I can't grasp a complete sentence, only the word "hospital." I look at their faces but they aren't speaking. The voice breaks off into gibberish as my head gets another jolt. "I think I need to... go. I appreciate..."

"...just relax," says the female. "We'll get you some help. If you leave now you may be in danger."

I look up at their pallid clinical faces and shudder. "I'll be... okay if I can... find my car and a friend who's..."

"...don't worry about that now."

I rise slowly while meeting their uneasy glances and step toward the door, keeping them in my periphery. The male springs for me as I reach the doorway and grabs my arm. I pull away and stumble into the waiting room, my pursuer close behind, and head straight for the exit. As I make it through the door the male tackles me to the ground, pins me face down, and cuffs me as we're surrounded by several other figures, including two security guards. I glance up on my left and see that the female interrogator is holding a white jacket in front of her like a shield. I swivel back flush and see two males in white coats pushing a gurney toward me. My head fills with static.

"This one give ya some trouble, doc?" quips one of the security guards.

"Nothing we can't handle."

"Take him up to Room 101?"

"Yes."

They strap me to the gurney face down and wheel me through the waiting room to the elevator, the faces of the patients-in-waiting pressed close to mine like they expect to find some inscrutable mystery in my eyes. When we get in the room—which is small and very bright with no windows—the security guards remove the cuffs and the two young males, who look like orderlies, wrap me in the white jacket. I can barely move my arms so I rock my body back and forth vigorously, thudding to the floor. From my vantage I glimpse a long table in the corner dense with instruments, but before I can get the complete view they pick me up and deposit me on a small bed in the corner with rails all around it. I keep fighting to break free from the jacket but they just laugh like I'm a defenseless rat caught in a trap. A large hypo seems to float in front of my face, driven by an unattached hand. The looks on the faces of the several observers seem suddenly very serious. The hypo disappears. I squirm and squirm but my efforts become more and more feeble.

"Relax, son, don't fight it. It'll only hurt your credit rating," says one of the blurry heads staring down at me.

It's another beautiful day along the beach. The clouds have just burnt off and the faces of the sun worshippers are euphoric. The tourists swarm along the boardwalk, chatting and snapping shots of almost everything they see, in search of the best place to score their midday morsel of nourishment and the most appealing trinket to validate their journey for friends and kin back in Bakersfield.

Near the corner of Breeze there's a building that's just been completed, a multistory, aqua-bluish-green marble structure with very few windows, all tinted. It juts way above all the other buildings on the boardwalk. On top of the building is a blackish, abstract serpentine structure that could be a sculpture commissioned by a bank, or a deflating cottage from a German Expressionist film set. It's difficult to tell from that far away. And when you move a few steps for a different vantage it seems to change shape. It could be a stylish postmodern penthouse, but there's no evidence of a human presence around it, only the butt of a pitch-black Cobra heli taunting the earthbound lookie-loos. A wall with upright, rectangle apertures positioned every ten feet or so rims the structure. A garden of antennae garnishes one side of the sculpture. Huge satellite dishes sprout at random from it, giving it a sci-fi film aura.

There's no name on the building, no lettering of any kind to identify its progeny. The front door is oversized and made of gray slate. Five security guards, dressed completely in black and adorned with the same logo that the three youths sported on the boardwalk, patrol the front area. Sitting up on a pedestal to the right of the door and near the boardwalk is a cage. It's about ten-feet high and six-feet square. There's a bench flush against the back side where a male sits gazing vacantly into the heavens. He seems oblivious to the passing stream but occasionally twitches as if a flicker of memory has briefly invaded his consciousness.

Hey, Momma, what's that man doing in there?" asks a little girl who breaks from the family chain to stare.

"Come on, sweetie," commands the mother, reaching back for her daughter's arm. "He's just... it's none of our business."

"But Momma, look... he moved. Is he looking at us?" The mother nestles up beside her daughter and the rest of the family falls in line, with the exception of the father who throws his hands in the air like it's another bothersome interruption in his life.

"No, I don't think so, sweetie." The mother begins waving her arms in front of her husband's face. As she stops, two of the slightly older children jump up in the air frantically, trying to reach the level of his stare with their flapping arms.

"There... he did, Momma!" says the little girl.

"Let's go," says the mother. "He's not interested in us and... Daddy needs to have his nap."

What's that... the screech... her arms. She's dancing. I need to follow her. The light is... too much. Don't stop... wait for me. I'm... no, no!

Fade to a soundless, dithering dark.

DISPOSSESSION

"This isn't Beverly Hills, Cedric! You haven't been here long enough to know what it's really like."
 "What would your family say about how you are... living here?"
 "What're you suggesting?"
 "Nothing... but you're right, it isn't Beverly Hills."
 "That's for sure," Segolene mumbles as she lets the towel drop to the floor and glides toward the shower, turning before she enters and flashing her emerald green eyes at him in what could be an invitation to join her cleansing ritual, but then says, "I gotta be somewhere soon... think my body's safe for now."
 What *would* her family say? Would they even be thinking about her one way or the other? How long has it been since she saw anyone in her family? A year at least. The last she heard was that her father had moved to La Jolla and her mother had moved in with one of the richest men in town, a guy she had been having an affair with on and off when Segolene was still living at home. She had the feeling, now that she thought about it, that she had been sort of disowned. But then she kept getting her monthly check. Solace enough. How would she survive if suddenly the checks stopped coming? Would she starve if she had to rely on her wits? She had few practical skills. Her father

never taught her finance—it just wasn't something a girl was supposed to know.

Her mother sent her to finishing school back east quite early, wanting to give her a disciplined environment away from male playmates while she, on the other hand, indulged in her own excesses. Her design was to turn Segolene into the kind of girl who could please a man with the right social resume and a cushion in the Caymans. Absolved from the need to work herself, she began early on to make sure her flesh and blood kept it all in the family, giving her a kind of map-of-the-stars mojo to follow. She dreaded the thought that her daughter could cultivate a colorful lifestyle and lose her blue-blood birthright in some urban blues scene and worse, bring home some layabout with no address.

Segolene was never quite sure what that school prepped her for. But she realized fairly soon that she would never be more than a work-in-progress at best. She refused to be finished off, wanted to be perpetually unfinished. All that pressured refinement for a life way in the future made her feel like she was a type being reproduced. She wasn't a rebel, exactly, but the moment came when the attempts to shape her at school no longer worked. She went home unexpectedly one weekend, discovered that her mother was dating a young stockbroker who dressed like a hippie, and endured a few weeks of intense questioning before emerging relieved, released from parental authority and free to mimic other behaviors. She set out on a series of journeys to discover new places and her mother, surprisingly, never seemed to mind.

When she finally made it to college it was adjacent to Venice, the beach town where she had already spent time during one of her escapes. After college she couldn't imagine returning to Beverly Hills and decided to settle in Venice, which promised to be safer and more interesting than downtown L.A.—it had become the trendy place to be for adventurers from Beverly Hills with bank accounts. Besides, it was close to home and she wanted to keep her parents happy.

In any case, if the checks stopped coming she could use her God-given talents and resume her full-time modeling career. It had been a pretty lucrative one, and she still freelanced. But she resented the pressures that came with it—to make porn films or become a prostie. She saw what happened to a couple friends who crossed the line. To stay with it they had to alter their minds and bodies and gradually withdrew from healthy relationships, becoming increasingly distant from their circle of friends.

She did consider making an erotic film with intimate acquaintances. But a friend once filmed a post-party romp at her place and she regretted it later. She liked to keep things private. From time to time she wondered what it would be like to be a working girl, not of the usual street variety of course. She knew she could be a dynamite above-the-bar, below-the-radar madam, but knew just as surely that she never would be. Just the knowing was enough.

She exits the shower, rejuvenated physically but a bit fagged mentally, like she's surfaced from a daydream where familiar forms are scrambled into an unfamiliar order, and decides to call her mother soon. Cedric has gone downstairs. She dries herself as she moves to a mirror but doesn't like what she sees. The light isn't right. She pulls herself away and shuffles across the spacious room to another one, hoping for more accurate illumination. This mirror, wider than the other one, seems to shorten her five-foot, eight-inch frame, which for the moment pleases her. She has harbored a sense of embarrassment ever since she could register her appearance as her own that she's too tall and too much, which in her mind means that she's not enough and not acceptable. But "normal" is unacceptable as well since she wants to stand out and be seen. She doesn't always know what standard to go by.

Modeling seemed to provide an instant solution. It justified her size and pumped up her confidence. But she didn't have a typical model's body and this prevented her from getting some of the top jobs when she was active and working more or less full time. Her breasts were too big, or so they said. They were disproportionate to her sleek body. Still there was nothing freakish about it, though she was often asked if she had implants.

It was her mother, whom she closely resembled, who had the true model's body. A blonde, light-skinned Nordic beauty, she was both slender and shapely with narrow hips that hardly reflected her post-childbearing condition and age, often guessed to be the mid-forties. Segolene got *her* breasts from her Italian father's side.

Despite having a body most women would die for—and a mother who appeared ageless—Segolene felt she didn't quite fit and became obsessed with perfecting her appearance. Nothing seemed to shake her fear of going rapidly downhill.

She secretly suspected her father's family as the cause. Their reunions were always fun events, with lots of eating and schmoozing. She liked a lot of the people she met but many of them didn't take good care of themselves and seemed slow. And reunions often included the surprise arrival of members no one had seen or even heard of before, strange characters resembling circus performers or gypsies who wandered from place to place with no special purpose, probably breeding like rabbits to become a subculture of claimants who pop up at the reading of wills. She romanticized their world at times, fascinated by the freedom these gypsies seemed to have, and wondered if she was harboring some irrational strain of wanderlust that polluted her gene pool. Could even one drop of blood be toxic?

She remembered reading once about a royal family that interbred with related bloodlines to expand the empire until its extended kin network eventually consisted mostly of babbling idiots, bringing down the entire kingdom. Was she destined to do idiotic things someday? Did her chemistry include a gypsy retardant?

This thought sends her to another mirror on the other side of this super-sized room. She needed as many different mirrors as possible to monitor her possible decline. These were of varying sizes and positioned at different angles to capture the most appropriate light. She was always measuring her hips against the image in the mirrors and trying to notice if she was getting a paunch so she could know whether to amp up her exercise routine.

At the moment it seems that her nipples are not as pert as they should be, so she moves down the wall to another mirror. She twists them with her fingertips, still moist from the shower, elongating and hardening them as much as possible to see how long they're able to conform. A slight grin begins to curl on her creamy pink lips, then a full smile as her green eyes become translucent, catching the light reflection off the mirror from a window on the side wall. She has been practicing her smile religiously ever since she did a commercial for a dental service several years ago.

She's thinking that she might need a nose job soon. It seems broader and somewhat flaccid compared to the last time she noticed. She had always been especially proud of her narrow, streamlined nose—a body part inherited from her mother—and the fact that to date she hasn't subjected herself to the knife. But would the moment of decline soon rush in, leaving her unprepared for the consequences if she didn't begin to take some precautionary steps? She flashes on the days when she did a lot of nude modeling. Exposing herself to an alien but titillated audience for a prolonged period always pumped her up, but afterwards she worried that she didn't look good enough. She decides to do a few exercises.

What should she wear? That's a no-brainer... everyone dresses the same at these... cocktail parties. It's the same people who show up and everyone talks about the same things. Who's hitting on whom? How much did so-and-so make last year flipping properties? It's like a reunion for real and imaginary exiles from Beverly Hills, or those looking for a ticket in. Almost everyone has slept with most everyone else at some point, though thankfully she has managed to be fairly selective about that. It's one big, incestuous kin group.

Not tonight... I can't. I need to get out in the open air, stroll around the streets and seek adventure. This urge comes every once in a while, but more and more lately. She gets such a rush from plunging into the unknown, dressing down, becoming anonymous like an undercover cop infiltrating groups for clues, not to criminal activity, but to the existence of kicks that can shatter the routines of everyday life. Her strolls are a form of fieldwork to learn new things about the city. She sees herself as an anthropologist investigating lifestyles that will one day become extinct.

She isn't so naïve as to believe she could find the naked truth through these sojourns, but she always feels in charge, like an artist with a palette varied enough to create a new masterpiece or the musician she once saw in concert who messed with a piano onstage for a long time as the crowd got antsy. A few people got up to leave but then some of the most unique sounds erupted that kept everyone suspended in wonderment.

As she ponders what to wear she smiles, musing that she could have been a quick-change artist in a carnival, consistent with her gypsy roots. She puts on her ripped and soiled jeans, faded Chuck Taylor tennies, Raiders jersey, and a crumpled army jacket a guy she brought home once left behind. Her costume is topped off with a long shaggy auburn wig she was given at a surprise birthday party.

Recently she has timed her strolls to coincide with the twilight hours, setting out as the sun is still bright but about to begin its daily disappearing act behind the water. As it descends the light becomes weak but also exhibits a spectrum of varying colors that kiss all bodies and objects with a special glow. They look different during this transition, truer and more natural. She reflects that this evening is especially striking, and not only because of the light. The sea breezes are sufficiently erratic to waft fresh odors between the buildings and across Speedway, neutralizing the peculiar smog smells. She feels like she's passing through a tunnel and imagining what awaits at the end.

"Otta my way lady!" a ponytailed male frame with determined eyes screams as he passes her in his wheelchair, nearly clipping her from the left side. He continues down the alley chortling demonically, an enlarged American flag flapping away on the back.

"Can't you give me fair warning?" she hollers, moving to the side of the alley.

After several more strides a hand reaches from around a dumpster and grabs her coat. "Ya got some spare change lady?" the owner of the voice squeals, a waif-looking character of indeterminate gender. Segolene swivels away in horror, as if to avoid some new strain of bubonic plague, and jogs to Westminster, stopping catty-corner from the Morrison Building to fantasize about its namesake who once lived there.

A couple of skateboarders breeze by her on the way to the boardwalk, miming an offer to bring her with them as a throng of Krishnas filing in from the sand breaks formation around her. She weaves through them and escapes to the fringes of a drum circle near the water, taking refuge in the soothing rhythms. The crowd of about thirty or so performs like one bongo-breathing organ beating the mystery chords of life. She moves around its edges to get a better look at the faces since the light is fading. A couple entwined in a bedroll is taking in the spectacle from the fringe.

Feeling extraneous, she decides to stroll south along the water. As she gains some distance the persistent drumbeats blend with the pounding of the waves in a pleasantly dissonant muzak and she forgets where she is until the sea supersedes the serial sounds. She welcomes the rush from the natural immensity of clapping violence at the edge of human awareness in a face-off with impersonal forces until three figures appear from about a hundred feet away, converting her euphoria to fear. She stops and the figures do as well. They exchange a few words before continuing toward her. She casually veers to the left, trying to pretend she doesn't see them while stepping up her pace toward the well-lighted boardwalk.

"Is that you, Aurelia?" the woman in the group shouts. "Where you off to?" Now within sprinting distance to the boardwalk, Segolene stops abruptly and turns around, curious despite herself.

"Got the wrong person... don't know anyone by that name."

"You look awfully familiar. I've seen you along the beach before. Are you looking for someone in our community?"

"Community?" Segolene inches closer to her questioner, beginning to feel less threatened by what she now recognizes as a woman's voice.

"The area from just south of here to where you see the mound above the water is our space," the woman responds. She moves within twenty feet or so of Segolene, trailed by two of the others with her, both males. "Are you curious about us? Is that why you wandered down here?"

"I'm just out for a stroll... breaking the monotony of..."

"...you came to the right place," says one of the males as the three surround her. "We offer ways to beat the rat race."

"Races are the last thing on my..."

"...we help people get off the street and find a better way to live than trying to be like everyone else... or trying to outdo them."

"I love the streets... it's where I find myself." Segolene sizes them up at a glance, tempted to make a break.

"You've nothing to fear from us," says the woman, reading her uneasiness.

"Why are you out here now? What..."

"...we've just had a meeting with our brothers and sisters living below the mound," says the other male. "Now we're headed to our safe house a few blocks away."

Segolene is not assured by his tone of voice. And races, getting off the streets, living below mounds... what's this all about? They talk like they don't belong here. She should call Mavis. Her people will know how to deal with them.

"Good luck getting back... hope you stay safe and..."

"...we can help you take charge of your life," says the first male, "be free of those who want to take advantage of you."

The light isn't cooperating, but she tries to get a clear look at him without being too conspicuous, shuffling a few inches to the left. He has a tight face, like he might be a minister or something. His words do sound like they're from a book. His voice is intimidating. He's wearing what looks like a military uniform but it's made up of uncoordinated pieces. Its condition suggests he has been in some kind of skirmish. She's normally turned on by uniforms but this one makes her feel uneasy.

"People are beautiful... I'm free, my own person."

"Let's bring her with us," says the second male, who's been eyeing her with disbelief. "She's too naïve to be true... must be a plant."

"That's a good attitude to have," says the woman to Segolene. "We have to believe in ourselves and others... but that's only a start." The woman now turns to each of her companions. "Let's back off and give her some slack... invite her to the house later."

"I'll take a rain check... don't think I could get into whatever it is you are up to, at least in this lifetime," says Segolene as she quickens her pace toward the boardwalk. "For the moment I'm hot on the trail of a good party if you can help with that."

The woman hollers an address at her, suggesting their get-togethers might be exactly what she's looking for. Eyes straight ahead, Segolene continues slogging through the sand. The second male wants to chase her down but the first one restrains him.

She reaches the boardwalk in front of Big Daddy's and glances over her shoulder but sees no one on the beach. Perhaps the fading light was playing tricks on her. She made no conscious effort to remember the address but somehow it sticks in her mind.

There's still a steady flow of activity on the boardwalk and it's well-lit so she decides to hang at Big Daddy's for a few minutes before moving on. This counter service-only fast food haven is a magnet for the area's nightly diversity since it's the only eatery open on this stretch of beach. There are tables and picnic benches in front and along the sides to accommodate the jaunting idlers, substance refillers, swarms of skateboarders fueling with chemical chili, wayfaring hookers attracting and repelling clients, the homeless negotiating a drink of water, ex-inmates from County in transit, sexual pre-daters, gangbangers, and a variety of other locals attracted to this scene like flies to a dead pigeon carcass.

A fair sampling of these are present this evening, including a few from the drum circle, a man in a tux chasing down an ice cream soda for his wife, a young woman in cowgirl getup meditating on a ketchup bottle, a young male jotting down notes on a menu, and a senior citizen reading a Ray Bradbury novel, *Death Is a Lonely Business*.

    Segolene peruses the menu items scrawled across the upper façade of the building while spying the activity inside the restaurant through the service portal, wondering how safe the food is. Figuring the question isn't worth an answer she orders a coffee and finds a perch on the northern edge, scoping the customers for signs. She picks up her own ketchup bottle and examines it, but it does nothing for her. A skateboarder cuts sharply across the boardwalk, stopping on a dime and freezing his frame for spare change. Perhaps her apparitions from the water will materialize.

    She notices the couple from the drum circle at the picnic table a few feet away feasting on chili dogs. They could be a couple of runaway kids, no older than their early twenties, perhaps throwback hipsters on the road to somewhere slumming in the niches of the recycled republic for the experiences that can get them out of it and lead to a more rewarding existence away from mainstream society. Or homeless wanderers without much of a clue, lost in the riptides of history and seeking ways to manage better in it. Who knows what happens to souls deprived. Do they perk up and get perceptive or dumb down? Much depends on whether they skinny-dip in the deprivation or get dunked by it.

    At the moment they're laughing and joking and soaking up the ambiance. They seem reasonably healthy though their skin is somewhat flat and turgid, attesting to some time on the street. Their clothing is frayed and soiled but it's not the usual surplus bulky hodgepodge of styles and seems to fit them fairly well. The girl is quite gaunt and possibly undernourished, but she could also be a borderline anorexic fashion model slumming it between gigs. Her affect seems to rule out substance abuse. She has long, matted blonde hair that's a few brushes away from coed respectability. He's tall and slender with long, dark-brown hair and a full beard and is also possibly undernourished. His hyper-active eyes suggest he might be under chemical influence.

As his girlfriend rummages in her backpack for something he starts to exchange looks with the cowgirl and stares at *his* ketchup bottle. The cowgirl's rapt gaze breaks into a blush. She picks up the remains of her hamburger special and proceeds to leave. Segolene observes the drama with interest.

"Hey, don't leave so soon," he says. "We aren't trying to get into your business. And we haven't had a chance to compare bottles." His girlfriend pulls out a crumpled piece of paper from her backpack while nodding in support and smiles at the cowgirl who hesitates before acknowledging the friendly gesture. But she continues to leave.

"You can use all the energy you got from that bottle to make good conversation," Segolene interjects, drawing a glance from the couple and arresting the cowgirl's progress. She turns to Segolene and then back to the couple, embarrassed by the triangulation.

"You guys together?" she asks.

"Nah, we're all strangers in transit," says the girlfriend.

"This seems to be the perfect place to be alone," interjects Segolene.

"Yeah, I come here all the time," says the

cowgirl, who now seems like she wants to hang a little longer.

"We're heading up the beach to crash in this van that a friend of a pal of ours parks near the sand," says the guy. "Trying to stay otta the alleys for as long as possible."

"You want to avoid that for sure," Segolene responds. "That's not good for your health." His fidgety eyes seem to be hiding something and this intrigues her. "Why don't we pretend like we're together? Come on over."

They slowly but eagerly accept her offer. The guy's thinking that he has seen Segolene somewhere. They're skeptical about a woman alone on the beach at night being friendly to them, but in a group there's not much to be afraid of.

As they sit down, Segolene gets a call on her cell. She thinks she knows who it is but can't bring herself to take it. Maybe they'll call back.

"Something wrong?" asks the girlfriend who's sitting to her left. Segolene's curious about her hair and tries to guess her age, thinking she's probably in her late twenties or early thirties. "Get some bad news?"

"No, nothing like that... just someone I hadn't expected to hear from so soon. I'll get it later."

The guy, who's sitting across the table, turns to the cowgirl on his left. "You got this thing about red? You like to spice up your burgers and French fries with..."

"...we caught her at an awkward moment," says Segolene. "Lighten up."

"No, that's... actually I hate the stuff... or I do now anyway. I used to pour it all over everything I ate almost, cuz I was tryin' to save money and someone said it had lots a nutrition in it. I didn't really believe that but I guess I sorta felt like it was true and... well, it made me feel better."

"So now you're trying to get it out of your system by staring at it?" Segolene asks.

"Or maybe she's still under its influence," quips the girlfriend.

"We don't mean anything," says the guy. "Just something to break the ice."

"But you guys must think I'm pretty weird though, huh?"

"Nah, I've survived on a lot weirder substances than ketchup for long stretches," says the girlfriend.

"Yeah, but you wanna get off that habit as soon as you can," says Segolene. "When did you have your last good meal?" She notices her pale complexion, fidgety mannerisms, and long black hair tucked under the cowboy hat that's not likely been washed for some time. Her accent, however slight, pegs her as a foreigner. She's dressed in recycled clothes that are a few sizes too large and give off a musty smell.

"I'm okay... recently moved in with some people and we've pooled our money and... hope it lasts."

"Know any other situations like that?" asks the guy. "We're in flux right now... came from a shelter off Rose. That's where we met."

"Not right now but... found mine at the Electric Lodge."

"We'll check that. Thanks!"

Segolene takes all of this in. This isn't exactly the thrill she was after when she dressed for the occasion. She feels apprehensive about revealing herself. Actually, she's not sure what to divulge. Something screens her from seeing them clearly, and it's not just their layers of neglect and fatigue. Her phone lights up again as they continue to chat. She tries to repress her anxiety and ponders what to do next. If she continues to refuse her calls they might get suspicious.

"You okay?" asks the cowgirl. "Something bothering you?"

"Yeah, you need a picker-upper," adds the girlfriend. "We bad company for you?"

"No, no... nothing like that. Just need to make a quick call and take care of some business. Always hate it when business interferes with pleasure."

She crosses the boardwalk to a bench on the fringe of the sand and pretends to make a call while they chat away. After a minute or so she crosses back over, projecting a credible air of relief. She's eager to get on with the evening.

"Well, that takes care of that, at least for the moment. If we could only tune out all the distractions from the world. Why don't we all continue our chat at my place? I live up the beach a few blocks."

"You aren't gonna kidnap us are ya?" the cowgirl asks with a grin.

"What kinda place you got?" asks the girlfriend cautiously.

"It's gotta be better than this place!" says the guy.

"Oh, it's just a... normal beach pad. I got it a few years ago when I moved here. And I'm not a kidnapper."

With her guests in tow, Segolene opens the front door to her condo.

"This is what you call a normal beach pad?" the cowgirl asks.

"What would your idea of *above* normal look

like?" the guy adds, looking at his companions with a glint of concern about what they might be getting into.

"Well... normal is what you make of it," Segolene responds as they pass through the doorway to face Cedric. He seems more upset than surprised, as if Segolene has violated some house rule. His expression quickly shifts to restrained forgiveness and the grace of a welcoming host.

"Let's head upstairs and relax for a while," she tells them. "This is Cedric. Cedric, these are some new friends. Don't know their names yet."

No one offers their name. Cedric reverses direction toward the hallway as she calls after him. "Bring us up some hors d'oeuvres, would you, Cedric?"

He doesn't answer but patiently watches them ascend the stairs, looking for some sign from Segolene. Getting none, he hustles to the kitchen, puzzled by something, and makes a quick call on his cell.

"So really, what's the story?" asks the guy. "Where does all this come from? What do you do to..."

"...so many questions! What difference does it make? Had a rich uncle who remembered me. He had this thing about cute little girls and we were close way back and..."

"...when's the last time you saw this wonderful person," asks the girlfriend as she collapses onto the capacious black leather sofa in the middle of the room and closes her eyes, appearing to nearly lose consciousness. "When do I get to meet him?" she suddenly asks, revived.

The guy begins to give himself the tour, glancing at the photos and art on the walls, paying special attention to the jewelry on one of her night tables. He appears to look behind the table for something and veers toward the mammoth bed, pancaking spread-eagle onto it. He lifts his head and meets Segolene's gaze through the mirror on the nearest wall.

"Comfortable?" she asks.

"I could stay here forever."

"Well, you're welcome to recharge your batteries for a while, but don't get too comfortable."

He rolls over and springs up, flashing a smile that's more like a squint and not directed toward anyone in particular, like when someone responds to criticism that they're not smiling enough and they try to oblige. He walks over to his girlfriend, looks into her face for signs of life, and steps around the end of the sofa, placing his hands on her shoulders which he proceeds to massage.

"You don't do any kinda work to pay for all a this?" the cowgirl asks from the other end of the sofa as Cedric enters and deposits a spread on a table near the door. The girlfriend is fully perked up and staring at him as if she's trying to recall who he is. He returns the stare before exiting.

"I keep pretty busy," Segolene responds, moving to the edge of her bed. "I'm part of a few neighborhood groups and do some acting and modeling, though less of it these days. I'm transitioning." The girlfriend meanwhile slips back into semi-consciousness and the guy moves next to the cowgirl and places his hands on her shoulders.

"Not for me!" she blurts, though apparently not too upset by his advances. She pulls away and moves to a chair closer to Segolene's bed. "I'm in transition too."

"We all are," says the girlfriend, "That's all people seem to do now."

"That's what makes it so exciting, right?"

Segolene chimes in.

"Not when the next thing won't involve a place to stay or enough to eat," says the cowgirl, eyeing the food.

"I'm transitioning to a better diet at the moment," the guy says on the way to the table.

"Gorge away everybody... help yourselves," says Segolene. The two girls hesitate and look around as if they're asking the room itself for permission to get up. Their reluctance softens as Segolene says, "I'll be back in a flash" and heads for the bathroom.

"The way the other half lives, huh?" says the guy to his two companions as they follow him to the table and begin to fill their plates.

"That's for sure," says the cowgirl. "You think she's wacko or somethin'? And I wonder who that guy is. Her mate... butler? Why doesn't he join us? I would love to get to know him."

"Yeah, see what you mean... but I've seen him somewhere," says the girlfriend. "And not too long ago either."

"*He* looks like most any sophisto with bucks," says the guy. "See that jewelry... and some of this art? *She* must be worth a fortune."

"He's gorgeous, but those eyes... the way he stares," adds his girlfriend.

"Maybe he's a psycho," says the cowgirl, trying to be flip but recognizing in the same moment that she may have spoken the truth as her eyes meet the girlfriend's. The guy just snickers.

"We'll be the subject of a Movie of the Week a few years from now," he says. "She'll seduce us... I hope she does... and throw us in the ocean so we wash up on some beach." His comments relieve the tension and they giggle away, the three of them getting closer now as a group.

"She doesn't seem the type," says the girlfriend. "She does seem kinda withdrawn though, like something's bothering her. Maybe that's the type we should be afraid of. "She reminds me of a mannequin I saw in a show over on Dudley about images of..."

"...how old you think she is?" asks the cowgirl.

"Old enough to know what she's doing," says the guy. "I'd just like to see what's under those clothes."

"We've only known each other for a short while and now you wanna start fucking someone else?" says the girl.

"Oh, I'm just playing!... what about you and that..."

Segolene exits the bathroom before he can finish, stoking his imagination further with her change of clothes and real blonde hair. She's dressed in casual denim and a loose-fitting top and is barefoot. With her makeup back on and her wig gone, she almost appears to be another person. She seems more relaxed and confident after a recharge in front of the mirror.

"Who's fucking who?" she blurts. "Not here. I decide who does naughty things like that. Anybody wanna wash up?"

With his eyes still on Segolene, the guy touches his girlfriend's arm and nods toward the bathroom but she pulls it away. Unfazed, he repeats the drill with the cowgirl. She refuses with a feeble smile. As he disappears into the bathroom, she wonders what his game is, and what his girlfriend would have done had she gone with him. She's glad to get some time with the lady of the house, this mystery woman who's trying to make them feel at home. She's beginning to perk up with the food, and a bath would be good even though she's kept pretty clean since she got her new living situation. What's their hostess got in mind next?

"Sorry about the outburst," the girlfriend says, inspecting the details of Segolene's appearance. "We really don't know each other very well. Even though we've been gettin' it on and seem to be very compatible, I don't have a claim on him. He'll probably come after you next. I'm not ready to hook up permanently anyway. Got gang raped on the street a while ago and he's been helping me get back into a confident physical relationship. I was mostly okay after it happened... got some therapy and stuff... but then just lost it for a while after that. I couldn't be with a guy... almost did myself in one night."

"Get as much out of him as you can," Segolene says in a motherly tone of voice. "That's what most of them are good for anyway. Get yourself off with tongue and cheek."

"That why you wear a wig?" asks the cowgirl. "Don't let them know who you are and stay uninvolved so..."

"...I like to try on different styles and experiment with new situations. It's a drag to look the same all the time and see the same people and do the same things."

"You seem like a free spirit too," says the girlfriend. "Maybe you're what I need. You can take him off my hands for..."

"...think I've seen that one before," Segolene remarks dryly as her cell goes off from across the room. She ignores it.

"Just kidding, but... well, I don't want to get dependent again. And I need to get otta this city, at least for a while."

"This marvelous town? Why?"

"I saw something on the street... or at least I

think I saw something but don't wanna be involved and... a friend may be in trouble cuz of it and... well, I think someone is following me too. That's why it has been nice to be with Eric. I feel safe. I've been wearing wigs too... and changing my name."

"What happened?" asks the cowgirl.

"Some guy got killed in this alley on the other side of Electric."

"And you saw it?" asks Segolene.

"Off the record, pretty sure but... was on meds then so..."

"...no future in being a good Samaritan," says the cowgirl.

"Someone will probably step up one of these days and... well, I'm gonna start reinventing myself anyway so... change my appearance, and my name."

"What name are you using now?" asks Segolene.

"Lately it's been Valerie. Not too original but it doesn't stick out and... it's a nice alternative to my real one, Willow. Actually that's not real either. It's my nickname but I've mostly always used it."

"Hey, what's going on with your servicer? Did he drown in there?" Segolene rises and motions toward the bathroom, tempted to check on her visitor, but goes for the phone instead to see who called.

"Ah, let him soak a little longer," Willow spouts, sensing she has sympaticos. A certain muted radiance seems to break through the silt of weariness and neglect with her words. The cowgirl inches toward her for a better look, seeing some color in her bleached gauntness that reveals her age more clearly. She guesses it to be at least twenty-five, possibly thirty, and wonders for a moment if she's really a street person. Are the anxiety and the lighting distorting the signs of deprivation?

Segolene sets the phone back down as Cedric taps on the door and enters, motioning her outside. Willow and the cowgirl exchange glances and take a mystery tour of the room. Both are wondering whether they should check on Eric as Segolene comes back into the room. She goes to the bar in the far corner and retrieves two bottles of wine, carries them to the table, and tells the girls to help themselves. They graciously oblige.

"I had a couple close calls on the street," says the cowgirl. "When I first came here from Mexico I was staying with some people at the park on Main and these two guys followed me there from work. I ran all the way and once they saw other people there they backed off."

"What were you doing?" asks Willow.

"Was strippin' at this club on Washington... all I could get once I got across the border. Got some education but it doesn't transfer, I guess. Wasn't really into it... grew up Catholic in rural Mexico and then not far from Mexico City and... if my parents ever knew! But I used this disguise on stage and also covered myself up as much as possible goin' and comin' so all the perverts would leave me alone. Was always afraid someone would recognize me from the club and bother me so I wore baggy clothes that..."

"...why the cowboy hat?" asks Segolene.

"Was part of my act at that first club I worked and kinda got used to it. All these cowboys went in there. Now I'm at a better place in West L.A. with more money where they escort you away from the club and... but I wanna get out of all that. Guess I'm good at it, but lots a women can be so..."

"...you gotta get otta that scene soon," says Willow. "That's a common story here. They'll keep pushing you farther."

"I'm definitely workin' on it. Some a the people I'm living with now are helping me. But it's hard to get references and the hours are kinda nice... and some a those guys out there in the audience seem so foolish. Kinda enjoy that. This new club lets you create your own costume so maybe I'm an artist. Used to study Rivera and Dali so... I'm using a cat costume now. This guy who used to come to my act every night said I had cat-like eyes. I even made up a new name for myself to go with it... Felina. My real name is Marisol but haven't used it for a long time. Seems better here to make things up. It gets you further."

"If you're getting better money, why are you living like you do?" asks Segolene.

"Been sending a lot of it back home to my family... they need it bad. Plus my mother says she has to send more and more of it to the local parish. Apparently the church needs it more than they do."

"Wow, that's amazing!" spouts Willow. "So you're religious?"

"Not really. Can't go to those churches anymore. Started doin' some Buddhism but stopped cuz couldn't stay focused on the things they said are important... but liked the feeling from meditating so I do that a lot but with just any ole objects around, like ketchup bottles. There! You kinda make up your church out in the streets every day. I started goin' to Big Daddy's cuz it was close to where I was hangin' and it was a good place to be alone and get away from all the people and noise. I think I'm becoming an atheist."

Willow and Segolene exchange baffled expressions but remain silent. Felina gets up from the sofa and walks toward the bathroom. But then she turns toward them, removes her cowboy hat, and pulls up her top. Her breasts are covered with feline tattoos. "My resume. What else am I qualified for?"

They ponder the question while absorbing how different she seems without the cowboy hat. Its removal released cascades of black, unwashed hair onto her shoulders that frame her tattooed flesh, an arabesque of tails, ears, yellow eyes, and protruding purplish nipples—incidental proof of her artistic aspirations. When she pulls her top back down they realize that her baggy clothes were hiding an awful lot of her.

Her efforts at disguise were successful. She'd managed to make herself look fairly average, so that getting a glimpse of her body relatively exposed makes her all the more interesting, inviting a refocus on her qualities through a different lens angle and f-stop.

Her legs are disproportionately long in relation to her upper body. Her facial expression, once the hair is no longer compacted beneath the hat, becomes more fervent, like she's getting a slight adrenaline rush from her revelations. Her blackish-green, luminous irises seem cat-like from the current angle of illumination. And when she moves her head slightly a nearly imperceptible yellowish sparkle can be detected, likely an illusion created by the lumens streaming from above.

"You could be qualified for lots of things," asserts Willow. "But... you're definitely qualified for... this." She blinks and looks away from Felina, who seems puzzled, but turns back toward her rapt with sympathy, secretly wanting another glimpse.

"There are many ways to use your talents," adds Segolene, who now sees a catlike movement in the way Felina looks at them, then veers off in a flicker of insouciance and unpredictability like the neighborhood feral yellow Tabby used to do when someone approached her.

The unveiling reveals a closer approximation to the girl's natural ethnic blend as well, trumping first impressions. She's far from the stereotypical, south-of-the-border Latina that the media gorges on. Her background is Mayan; she hails from a village in Chiapas. But she diverges from that short and stocky style because her great-grandmother married a tall German officer during WWI when his country provided military assistance to the Mexican army trying to defeat Zapata. Felina's a visible throwback to these origins, a living genetic surprise with a Teutonic bone structure and much taller and more slender than her five siblings. This mixture leaves her looking older than her nineteen years.

Yet the socio-economic life of the rural, Mexican peasantry dictated her mannerisms, movements, and dress—qualities that did not mix well with her Nordic attributes during her formative years. But here and now she has a chance of synergizing where survival requires adaptation. She could evolve into a new species of urban being, a well-bred physical goddess mated with a nomadic, spiritual gypsy working her plan for salvation in the cracks of our modern body factories.

She confidently turns around and walks to the bathroom.

Stretched out in Segolene's mammoth tub, Eric stares at his beard and wig on the commode. He relishes the chance to soak, to rinse away the dirt from his days on the street, and welcomes the chance for transparency. When can he get rid of the name and props? He wonders what they're schmoozing about in the next room. You never know who you might bump into on the streets. *I could get into living in these digs,* he muses. *She's got more than enough for the rest of us. She's the boss. These are the people who call the shots. I wonder what's behind that door.*

The bathroom proper is some distance from the entrance. The space between is a sort of anteroom, nearly the size of his studio apartment on Breeze. It includes a love seat and two chairs and the walls are plastered with photos and paintings. *Not a bad place to ponder your fate before taking a plunge. Is that a closet? Perhaps it contains some of her skeletons. A room off of a room that leads to a bathroom—I thought I'd seen everything. What am I going to do about... Willow, or whatever her real name is? She's bound to open up one of these days, especially if she finds more babes to chatter it up with. They're probably pumping her for information right now. Boy, would I like to pump the lady of the house! What's something like that doing at Big Daddy's, especially at night? She must be working for somebody. Or maybe she's a funky working girl. I'll have to settle for the cowgirl. I love westerns. No, gotta stay focused on Willow. Have to follow up with the cowgirl later, unless we can get some wild scene going here. Maybe the lady of the house is a puppet master. Make that mistress!*

He reluctantly lifts himself out of the tub and contemplates his beardless face and short, disheveled hair in the mirror. *It's refreshing to see the real me. All this pretense makes me forget who I am.* The smells excite him. Is it her perfumed body that cuts through the soapy water or the fresh flowers wafting from the corner of the room? He imagines her in the mirror beside him, undressing. *Well, I can fantasize, can't I? Once you stop doing that you're finished.*

He puts himself back together, inhales a final

wisp of her fragrance and enters the anteroom. *Should I try that door?* He looks around the room briefly and then decides to. It opens to a dark hall with no windows and extends straight ahead for some distance but he can't see the end. Should he follow it? He looks back into the anteroom and at the door that leads into Segolene's bedroom and creeps forward a few feet. He still can't see the end but notices another passageway off of this one that turns left. What if someone shuts the door behind him? He takes a few more steps and peeks around the corner. This corridor seems identical but shorter, and there are a few specks of light on the near wall that brighten the space somewhat. This allows him to see a couple shelves on the far wall that are filled with what appear to be files. He looks for a light but can't find one. At the end of this hallway there's another door. Still worried about being shut in, he retreats back to the anteroom and collapses onto the love seat. A tap on the door. He scrambles back to retrieve his coverings just in time to face Felina, who enters the anteroom smiling. Barely recognizing her, he does a double take.

"You about clean enough? We thought you drowned in here."

"Who... you musta... where's your cowboy hat, sister?" he responds, flustered by her appearance but jacked up by her presence.

"Who needs it? You gonna let a girl clean up?"

"All yours... just been trying to keep the pleasure going as long as possible."

Willow enters the room, stifling all fantasies. "You've had enough of that for a while." She grabs his reluctant hand and escorts him into the bedroom and onto the sofa, where he lounges back and gazes at the ceiling. The soak and the discovery of the mystery hallways and the erotic charge from Felina have left him in a reflective reverie. And cleaned up he seems more vulnerable—he's lost the commanding stare and swaggering assertiveness.

Willow has never seen him like this. Segolene, who's been observing him closely in anticipation of mental fisticuffs, enters his field of vision but fails to break the trance. She moves around behind the couch and begins massaging his shoulders.

"Hey, cowboy, what did you see in there?" She grins at Willow and backs away as Felina enters.

"See how quick women can be!" She walks over to the food table and pours a glass of wine as Eric snaps out of it and Willow rushes into the bathroom. Refreshed and radiant, Felina stretches out on Segolene's bed. Segolene pours a glass of wine for herself as her cell on the table starts beeping. She doesn't answer but picks it up and moves to the door. She opens it quickly and Cedric backs away sheepishly; he's been listening. They head down the hallway together.

"What's going on here?" Eric asks Felina. "What's her story?"

"You got me. Maybe she likes to help people."

"Have you noticed the look in her eyes? She's up to something."

"But it can't be bad. She probably just wants to reach out to a different group of people."

"Why would she want to be around us?"

"Speak for yourself. Don't you feel worthy of her attention?"

"I feel I should be... I am... I want to be around her, believe me."

Willow enters the bedroom, glistening with confidence and chemicals from Segolene's preserve and wrapped in one of her robes.

"You gals are awfully quick," says Eric. "Afraid you'll miss something"

"Did she show you her tits yet?"

"No, not... what have *I* been missing out on?"

"Want me to?" asks Felina. "You don't want him to be left out do you?" she continues sarcastically while looking at Willow and then at Eric for a sign. She breaks the silent tension by lifting her top very quickly and forcing her breasts in front of his face and just as quickly dropping it. "See enough? You guys get so lathered up by such trivial things."

"No, I haven't seen enough."

"Okay." She takes her top off and throws it on the chair. "Why is this such a big deal? Did you have some trouble when your mother breastfed you?"

"Now that I think of it, I might of... and my mother hated cats," he stutters, trying to get his flow back.

"Don't egg him on... he'll freak out," says Willow. "Put it back on."

"Don't listen to her. I'm fine with it. She's just jealous because she doesn't have what you got."

Willow's tempted to prove him wrong, and he knows that he is. But she doesn't want any part of this game. She can't handle it. It rekindles the emotions associated with her rape, emotions she has been fairly successful at managing lately. Her cosmetic sheen now seems to vanish and her expression shrink-wraps, leaving her confidence as deflated as Felina's crumpled top.

Felina, meanwhile, moves away from them and finds the mirror on the far wall, drawing Eric's attention; he spies her cats through the glass as she preens away. Willow watches Eric for several seconds, and looks out at Segolene coming up the stairs leading to the deck. She comes back inside, looks at Felina, then at Eric, and then at Willow, trying to decipher the meaning of this new constellation.

"Hey, who changed the dress code?" she asks Felina while staring at Eric. "You guys inventing a new relationship?" She walks across the room, picks up Felina's top, and brings it to her chest, hanging it on her nipples. "Don't you get enough practice over at the Pussy Lounge, or whatever they call it?"

"I'm comfortable with any code you got," she responds, putting the top back on. "He wanted another look so thought I would be neighborly, especially since we're spending so much time here together." Eric backsteps to the sofa and looks beseechingly at Segolene like he hopes she'll renege.

"Well, I'm not really for any dress code... it's not that. I just wanna make sure we stay friendly and honest."

While Segolene plays pacifier, Willow opens the door to the deck and closes it carefully behind her, relishing the escape into the night air and the smell of the sea breezes. Why did he have to spoil everything? They were getting along and she hadn't felt like this in a long while. The thrill of new people in a different place! The view from above, it's refreshing. She spends so much of her existence down below, at street level, feeling oppressed by it. Looking down now at some of the spaces she's occupied gives her a sense of security and control, like she's found some sort of sanctuary. But it's not real. *I belong down there.*

She inches toward the rail. I'm doomed. I'm sure someone is following me. Ever since that murder my life has changed. Everyone has scattered. She's lost touch with friends and acquaintances, the contacts that want to help her get off the street. She hasn't seen her friend who has been accused. She has to, but she's afraid what that will bring. She needs companionship, a family. She breathes in more of the natural elements, getting dizzy from them, and reaches for the rail. She looks down and sees a shape starting a fire in the alley, wondering if it's someone she knows. Then a loud crashing wave beckons her toward the water.

"Admiring the sights?" asks Segolene, her sudden presence muting the effect of the vista, drawing Willow slightly back from the rail. Willow composes herself before turning full-face toward her host.

"Guess I lost touch with myself for a few minutes there. Just being up here gets you to think about things in ways you usually don't. I could really use a place like this at the end of every day. You've sure got a great view."

"You're awfully close to the rail. Sure you're okay?" Segolene sees through her attempt to feign a cheerful mental state. "Here, take my hand. Let's go inside and join the party."

"Some party."

"Don't mind him... no one else is."

She hesitates, like a gust of wind or a seagull soaring by could send her back flush against the rail. "I've got lots of things on my mind."

"Don't we all." Segolene reaches her hand out again and moves closer to Willow, taking care not to be too abrupt.

"I'll be down in a few minutes... need more time to..."

"...what's that gonna do for you now?" She touches her hand "Come back up later if you want." When Willow's hand clasps hers she guides her away from the rail.

After a few steps, Willow pulls her hand away. "I'm okay. Let's go down."

The scene below is not what Willow expected. Eric is lounging on the sofa, his right leg straddled over the top, chatting with Felina who's miming one of her performances fully clothed in front of the mirror, partly for him and partly for herself. He's trying to convince her to do one of her acts in the flesh but she just beams him a periodic smile and continues with her pastiche.

"Why don't you get up off your butt and do one yourself ?" she tells him, then turns to the new arrivals. "We'd love to see that, wouldn't we girls?"

Willow responds first. "It wouldn't be a very big deal, believe me. I can give you a pretty good picture if you want."

"Not for me," adds Segolene. "I think I have a pretty good idea already." The other women do an interior double take. Under other circumstances she would have seduced him already. He captivated her down at Big Daddy's—a tall mysterious creature from the darkness at the edge of... normal civilization. She could have snatched him away from the girls easily. She still could. Should she? She could teach him a lesson at least, but the erotic charge is fading. Why? Too much light... exposure? Too much trivial conversation between all of them over too long a time? Familiarity breeds suspicion and this can lead to a contempt that flags the sex drive. The art of seduction is about being impersonal, avoiding intimate attachments, and that means managing the experience as quickly as possible.

One of the most stimulating physical experiences she ever had was with a guy she found in a happy hour at the Canal Club. She'd only known him for a few minutes, just long enough to know he was extremely attractive and for her imagination to take over. They darted over to his studio in the ether of anticipation, ravaging each other in the dark for several hours, and happily parted ways, not wanting further contact. As always, the thrill of victory came from speed and the chance to dictate terms.

Who was the guy in that film? Frank somebody. He forced his mates not to look at him while he inhaled some drug from a see-through cup and fucked them.

She did some soul searching after that. Thankfully, though, she never reached the point where she has had to be drugged. So far fantasy has served her well.

The girls, strangely, are more appealing than him. Their energy and concerns have taken over and this has made him seem different. But this bothers her. Why did she have to invite all of them? She needs to put the day in reverse. This illusion has to be shattered so she can get back to what she does best. Steal him away and... get it over with. These girls are cramping her style, clouding her vision. What's so interesting about them? She's tempted to show her tits to Felina and the other two. *That stripper's got nothing on me.*

"Why don't you go to Willow and talk her into stripping for us," says Felina.

"No, no... he's seen it and I'm sure you girls could care less what I... I think I'm going into hibernation soon... start covering myself up more. Maybe I'll head off to the convent and finally make my parents happy."

"Okay, girls, you win. But you can't blame a guy for wanting you to do what comes natural." The expression on his face suggests he feels they *are* blaming him. He gets up and walks around the room.

They watch him, expecting some further comment, and finally lose interest, chattering among themselves as he pauses at the table on the other side of the room where pictures and pieces of jewelry are scattered randomly.

"What're you girls gonna do?" Segolene asks. "Moving around and living with different people while stripping for strangers in sleazy clubs... there's no future in that... and it's dangerous. There are better ways to display your gifts. This moving from shelter to shelter with Mr. Reliable and spending time on the streets... it's threatening out there. Lots of people are getting aggressive about cleaning the area up. And lots of people on the streets are getting violent, even killing each other. Seeing murders and being followed and... There's a war going on."

Eric perks up at the allusion to him and shuffles away from the jewelry, trying to catch snippets of their conversation.

"You think we have a choice?" responds Willow. "You've got all this to keep you safe and content, but it's another world from the one we live in. Not everyone can live like you do. You have the freedom to do lots of things and... ignore what happens on the streets."

"You *can* get away from it... you *do* have some choice," says Segolene.

"Just say no to the street... just like that?"

"No to living on it... staying out there overnight and..."

"...we're open to a plan." says Felina.

"Why are *you* so fascinated by the street?" asks Eric as he steps around behind Segolene, placing his hands on her shoulders while ogling Felina as if to tell her he's found someone who appreciates his touch.

Segolene turns toward him with an emotionless expression and then back to Willow, letting him continue.

"I... like to pay attention to... what happens out there. I'm always out circulating and... love to look at faces and see..."

"...but you don't have to stay out there," blurts Felina, "and... especially overnight. Ever tried that? I haven't done that too much myself, but..."

"...if you find the right places and do it with the right people. I stayed with this guy on the beach through part of the night once, not far from the pier."

"But that's not the same," says Willow. "And what do you get from passing through sleazy restaurants in the early evening?"

"Thrills in facing the unexpected... meeting lovely new people like you guys... having new experiences. It stokes my imagination!"

"Then you come back here and have these thrills in the privacy of your mansion," inserts Eric as he inches his fingers down below her collarbone and slightly under her top.

"I get the good without the bad... why's that a problem?"

"It's not a problem," says Felina. "I would love to do that... avoid the bad stuff."

"But do you get either?" asks Willow. "If you hung out there in the alleys and in the parks and on the beach overnight for a while you might learn why people are on the streets and what they're looking for that's... different from what most people want."

"I know what she wants," says Eric. "Some excitement she's not getting somewhere else. Why did you really bring us here?"

Willow is becoming uneasy with Eric's

maneuvers, shifting her looks between his plunging fingers and Segolene's expression, which is now evincing glints of budding rapture. Her stare ineffective, Willow rises and moves around behind him, pulling his arms back. Segolene takes a deep breath and shifts her legs.

"Just returning a favor to a lovely lady," he says with a smile, one that Willow at least sees through. Eric pulls her gently to the sofa and smooths her hair.

"See, he can be nice," announces Segolene. "Should we be nice to him, girls?" No one answers. "Okay... okay. He's not ready to be initiated into our experimental family."

"I am," he says, "but Willow doesn't want me to be."

"And neither does Felina, apparently," returns Segolene, "so we'll leave it at that for the moment."

"Why did you bring us here?" repeats Eric. "You don't *really* want us to hang out with you... be your friends... do you?"

"We met in a public place and it was magical and... we're sort of hitting it off and... we're just feeling each other out now. Who knows, this could be..."

"...do you want to keep us as your slaves?" asks Felina sarcastically. "I won't resist... especially if your bodyguard is the slavemaster."

"Keep you as... no, nothing like..."

"...you wanna be like us?" asks Willow. "Do you see yourself in us?"

"Aha, that's why I like you girls. You're sensitive to things. I think that's close to the truth. I spent some time travelling around when I was your age and... maybe I left something back there that..."

"...you wanna have sex with us?" asks Felina. "Are we all gonna be a very happy family in your big bed before we go... with your bodyguard joining us?"

"No, that's not... you guys are welcome yourselves but... I'm attracted to you, but not in that way. As for Mr. Quickfingers," she says, addressing the girls, "I... could've been but he's got this attitude. He gets me hot for a moment, then he opens his mouth and my body becomes dry and frigid, stiffens with head stuff."

Eric's own body stiffens as she speaks. His eyes bulge out and he gets up, too frazzled to speak, and rushes toward her, stopping in his tracks when they're face to face. "What're you talking... how can you say that?"

She turns and smirks at the girls to get their reactions. He reaches for her top, pulling it even with her head before she breaks away and circles round the sofa to her cell, holding it aloft.

"See what I mean?" If you hadn't opened your mouth... just let your body do the talking and... taken me. If you were worth it you would've known what to do with me and when. I don't like to wait. And you're like a rapist, into forcing... you can do damage to people."

He's speechless. The girls stare at him and he sits back down on the sofa, withdrawing like a scolded child.

"That's why it's gonna be hard to be a family... he messed it up. Maybe we can get someone else. Know another stud, girls? I can be your mother... a chaperone that makes sure we all evolve in..."

"...maybe your bodyguard can join us," says Felina.

"No, Cedric's off limits... he'd be bad for you... he *is* bad... and you're too young. He serves my purposes though... perfectly."

"Okay, mother!"

"Can we still do something with *him*?" asks Willow. "Is he salvageable? I can't think of any recruits offhand." She glances in Eric's direction but he remains withdrawn.

"We'll see how he takes to our group therapy." Still no response.

"We're going to have... therapy?" asks Felina excitedly.

"Not in a clinical sense just mean continuing our moment here, our experiment, seeing what we want, why we're here and "

"...you do sound like a therapist," says Willow. "I've been through that before and... I have more confidence in you than the others."

"We all want the same things," says Felina, "companionship and... money to do what we want to do... though I haven't had much of a chance to find out what that means."

"Money doesn't mean that much to me," says Segolene.

"Yeah, now that you have so much of it," says Willow. "If you hadn't had it you couldn't have done that travelling. We all wanna survive and be happy but if you lack money and smarter minds make it hard for you "

"...it would be nice not to have to worry about money at all," says Felina. "Don't really care for the people who have it, though. You get into some interesting situations on the street. Lots of the people out there seem more honest. You learn things out there from them."

"I'll vote for the money!" spurts Eric.

"I agree," says Willow. "Money isn't the answer and, in my experience, anyway, the people you have to deal with when you're around it don't stimulate me." She glances at Eric, who's gone back into his cocoon. "There were these two friends, a guy and a girl, who hung with us for a while and they were really cool, always helping people and open and... one of them got this inheritance and they were gone... I woulda been too... but they became totally different. We'd see them somewhere after that and they looked at us like we were scum. But another friend came to the street after he had a really good job and money and a house and a great girlfriend and... at first he was cold and mean and then everyone was going to him for advice and help and... he became a different person."

Segolene shakes her head. "You guys are just trying to make all that seem good so you won't feel like you wasted your time out there."

"It's a wasteland out there for sure, even if you ignore all the pigeon crap," says Willow, choosing her words carefully. "I want to say that the people on the street aren't doing the killing. They're the victims. I don't know everything that's going on out there these days but the trouble's coming from outsiders... people we never saw before appearing all over and... well, the street people can get pretty aggressive sometimes and there's definitely problems but they don't kill each other. No one of our group raped me, I'm sure of that. I was on medication because of it but I am pretty sure now that my friend wasn't around when that guy was killed."

Eric suddenly snaps out of it, seemingly disturbed by what she said. She rushes over to him, collapsing on his lap, and starts to stroke his leg, which soon degenerates into giddy play.

"Slow down there," says Segolene. "That's not the therapy I had in mind but... you guys can use my bed if you want."

Eric stops and looks up at their benefactor. "When are you going to do therapy with me, doc, so I can be a member of the family?"

Willow jumps up from his lap. He reaches for her arm in a gesture of apology but she manages to twirl away.

"Let's go up on the deck," Segolene whispers to Felina, let them go at it. If she satisfies him we might be able to make some progress... or at least get him off our tails for a while."

The air on the deck is cooler than it was earlier but a cloud of humidity seems to have nested in the area and altered the smell of the sea breezes. They stretch out on the lounge chairs and take in the view, content to enjoy a speechless interlude for a change. After several minutes they hear a series of muffled groans that surge toward a crescendo that doesn't arrive, followed by absolute silence.

"See what we're missing?" says Segolene, breaking the ice. "Should we join them?"

"Well, let's give 'em a little more time first," returns Felina, clearly relaxed enough to do just that.

"How did you get those cats and... why?" asks Segolene. "Why not keep your natural color? I've been trying to get my tits perfectly bronzed forever. I lay up here and on the roof but it takes so much time and there's always some pervert with binocs checking out the equipment. You already got 'em."

"I don't know... the guy where I was dancing, as I mentioned, said I had cats eyes and so I went for the look, and I like cats too and got tired of the same ole color and got a good deal from this other guy, so... why not? And I kept 'em cuz the boyfriend I had then said they excited him a lot... they made my nipples seem extra large. And he was so into them, sucking them all the time like he was a little baby breastfeeding. That was kind of a thrill but he could be really rough sometimes. He loved dogs and had a canine personality and was always... why am I saying all this?"

Segolene's expression turns reflective and she pulls her top up. "How would mine look with tattoos?"

Felina is startled, not expecting this exposure, but quickly recovers and stares at them like they're a rare sculpture. "How do you keep 'em so full and firm? You're about thirty, right?"

Segolene proffers a self-satisfied smile. "Thirty-nine."

"You're kidding? Your skin is amazingly well-preserved." Felina's excitement transits to a slight movement of her hands, suggesting she might want to touch them. "How do you keep 'em like that? I'm only nineteen but I wanna learn good maintenance early."

"You seem a lot more mature physically than nineteen."

"I developed early... became aware of my body and sex at about eleven."

"That can be a blessing or a curse. I work at it constantly... lots of exercises, diet. It helps to get them touched a lot by someone you want to touch them."

"I have a hard time keeping hands off mine."

"That's the curse," says Segolene as a mild scream interrupts them, succeeded by several seconds of silence. After several more seconds it recurs, ratcheting through a series of piercing sonorities to what seems like the threshold of pain, then silence again. A sound finally erupts which is difficult to identify since it is overlaid with a string of broken words.

"Well, it seems like Willow's doin' okay," says Felina.

"I hope so. Anyway, Cedric has a lot of things he does with his hands that help. He has a canine personality too, by the way, and can be... well, he definitely likes my tits pure and white."

"What's the story with him? Thought he was your butler or something but..."

"...our relationship is complicated. We have very similar backgrounds and come from the same area. He's my bodyguard, but he takes care of my body too. We're extremely compatible physically, but we aren't romantically involved. He brings women here and I bring men—and sometimes older boys. I guess you could say we service each other. It's a wonderful, mutually beneficial relationship."

"Can I meet him? Think he'd like me?"

"Yeah, he'll definitely... but no... as I said, you're too young. Why don't you stay here, at least for a while... get away from that life you've been leading... the street people. There's no future in that scene. With your qualities you should definitely expose yourself, but to a different class of lookers. You also need to completely get rid of your accent and... whiten up.

"But you said I should keep my natural brown color and..."

"...not... that brown. The lighter the better for your... future happiness."

Felina looks at Segolene, who's staring off into the heavens. She's confused by the comment and wants to respond, but falls back into her chair, modeling Segolene's pose. They both remain in the same position for several minutes.

"Think it's safe to rejoin our friends?" Segolene asks suddenly.

"I'm ready if... they are," says Felina.

All the lights in the room are out except for a nightlight in the far corner, and no movement can be detected. "Maybe they aren't ready," whispers Segolene. "Should we mount a surprise greeting?"

"Yes... yes, let's mount 'em!" Felina whispers back.

Segolene thinks she sees shapes on the bed. "Should I turn the lights on?" Felina shakes her head.

Stepping farther into the room, Segolene drifts into a smell that's quite striking since her lungs are still filled with sea air. Is it from their sweating bodies, she wonders.

Felina suddenly spurts ahead of her and leaps onto the bed, her head coming to rest between two legs. She pulls back and looks up into the face of an unrecognizable figure and jerks back, repelled by the same smell. Segolene takes a few steps to the side and hits the light switch. As the room is illuminated Felina screams and hustles backwards until she's against the wall. Segolene stoically eyes the figure.

It's Willow, wearing a wig with a string of hair wrapped tightly around her neck, her nude body propped up against the headboard. Staring blankly into the room, she resembles a mannequin waiting to be dressed for display.

Disabled momentarily, Segolene walks swiftly to the bed. Thinking she perceives some slight breathing she rushes into the living room and opens the door, shouting for Cedric. Getting no response, she hustles to the table along the far wall, picks up her cell, and calls 911.

THE ASSIGNMENT

Sonny lies semiconscious on the sofa, his head angled down from the edge and inches from an oak coffee table that suddenly begins to vibrate. He stares at his cell as the vibrations travel along his sightline to his head like an electrical current that causes it to start throbbing. He misses the call, but the throbbing persists so he retrieves a few Norcos scattered across the table and washes them down with what's left of a bourbon and water. He waits a minute or so and fingers the cell, trying to compose his lines, but has difficulty choosing the best narrative from the rush of options and kills the call. Falling back on the sofa he ponders his defense but soon slips into slumber until jolted by the doorbell.

In the seconds from the sound to the return of his sense of time and place he tries to retain his musings—his not-fully-formed dreams—since he hadn't been under long enough to slip below the gate, though he was near enough to it. It's one of those moments when your concerns acquire such intensity that they follow your plunge and edit themselves into a story so you can make sense of them—but here it dissolves into a fuzzy treatment.

He dithers in the sound waves of the bell. Have they come after him already? How does he confront these faceless, voice-distorted shadows? Should he duck out the kitchen window and run like hell? But to where? To what? He reaches between the sofa cushions for his 9-millimeter, caressing the cold steel like it's a lifeline to redemption, then tosses it to the edge of the sofa like its mere presence in his sweating hand sends a shock wave through his body. The bell rings again, this time longer, and repeats one more time. *Stay absolutely still and they'll go away.*

Nearly a minute transpires and he takes a deep breath, wanting to feel relieved, aware that his headache is nearly gone. Should he get up and move around? Before he can answer in the affirmative, the intruder presses the bell several times in succession, but they're not evenly spaced strikes. The time between one and two is quicker than that between two and three; the time between three and four is slower and the time between four and five is very rapid.

He loses himself in the dissonant melody, but then realizes it could be a code. He wishes he could hear it again. Pain surges through his right lobe, causing him to lie back and takes a deep breath. Should he know this code? Is he too suspicious? Has he been warped by his clandestine existence?

He stretches along the sofa and grabs his weapon again, giving the intruder one more chance to leave. After several seconds he hears a voice he doesn't recognize and he can't make out the words. It seems to be coming from a different direction and farther away. He hears his name pronounced from what now seems like a closer distance and, realizing that the intruder isn't going away, marches to the door. He opens it carefully, holding his weapon in readiness.

His glimpse of the visitor puts him further on the defensive since he doesn't recognize him, and he comes close to letting him have it. The man comes quickly through the door, his movements suggesting he's been here before. As he passes into the living room Sonny begins to make the connection, observing that the intruder's normally business-like detachment is mussed with personal affectation, his body language an inchoate preface to a work in progress. Is he being pursued by someone? Then the man's face relaxes into a familiar configuration and his words fall into place.

"Hey, what's with the iron? You don't really think..."

"...just a... precaution, Mr. Jones. Your voice must've changed or something."

"You didn't pick up and... well, we really shouldn't talk on the phone, anyway, so I decided to drop over... don't want to risk anything at this stage."

Sonny gestures him to a chair as he plops down on the sofa and tosses the piece just beyond his outstretched arm.

"What... stage? What do you mean?"

"You okay? Remember our..."

"...I... I fell asleep and... got a headache that comes and goes but sometimes I can't... but you probably know about that already, right?"

"Know about what? Don't you remember we had a meeting set?"

"When? Who sent you?" Sonny refuses eye contact, stealing a glance at his weapon like he's afraid it might disappear.

"What do you mean who sent me? Are you sure you're okay?"

"Are *you* okay? You don't seem the same as... when did we last meet?"

"Oh, come on? What's happened? You're not okay!"

"No, I'm okay for now... just popped a few pills. We'll see."

"When? You get headaches often?"

"Got in a rumble with this dude and he got... lucky. But I'll get it all sorted out in due course. I can get some substances from my therapist."

"Sure you don't need a doc?... can refer you to one of our people, no questions."

"I'll see how I feel later. I'd be down for the count by now if it was that bad. Takes more than that to..."

"...what sort a rumble was it? Thought you were going to avoid too much exposure. Gonna be ready for an assignment?"

"I was wondering about what you said last time and... didn't really understand what that was all about."

"That's all changed. We got some new players and the roles of some of the old ones aren't all that clear now."

"Who's we? Who's behind what we've been talking about these past weeks? I mean, who do you take orders from?"

"You gotta be kidding! We went over all this weeks ago. Don't you remember?"

"Refresh my memory."

"The woman... member her? You got some papers at her place and..."

"...member some papers but... what'd she look like?"

"You told me!"

"What'd I say?"

"You said she was a real babe, had lots of money, great pad, and... you stayed at her place and she had a bodyguard. Wait a minute, you playing some kinda game?"

"Wouldn't forget something like... who told

you to tell me to do what I did?"

"Uh... we'd straightened all that out. You must've gotten hit pretty hard. Maybe we should get you a doc."

"No... I'm alright. Maybe a little fuzzy but..."

"...okay, well that woman's been... how can I put this... you can forget her for the moment. We've got another situation we want you to handle."

"Who's we?"

"The... what do you mean? We talked about this."

"Who you working with who wants me to do this?"

"I work with more than one person... you know that."

"I only remember you talking about one... a dude you worked with before and told you he knew me and some of the people I'd worked with when..."

"...he's the guy who did intelligence work in the military. He's still in the picture."

"But... if there are some new players and the roles of some of the old ones aren't as clear, then are we still in the same ballgame? We still fighting over the same things?"

"Of course! It's just that the situation has changed somewhat. I can't discuss it right now, but trust me. We're on track."

"To do what?"

"What needs to be done... we discussed that."

"Everyone still on the same side?"

"There's nothing to worry about!" Mr. Jones snaps, his confident directness belied by a barely perceptible flinch that causes Sonny's gun arm to twitch on the sofa. "Nothing whatsoever."

"What are the sides?"

"You gotta be kiddin' me! You of all people, who can sniff out injustice like a connoisseur can smell the bouquets of fine vintage wines... all the dirtbags who have nothing better to do than harass and kill the good people. You lost sight of who you are? I had you figured for a true warrior... a warrior who would never quit."

"I ain't no quitter once I get the message and people tell me right." Sonny's expression contorts into a coiled spring. "I don't like hypocritical assignments."

"Always been up front with you... never steered you in the wrong direction or given you false information."

"You friends with a Mr. Smith? He one of your new players... playing a new role for you?"

"What are you talking about? This some kind of joke? You watching too many old movies on the tube?"

"You guys with your names... that's the joke. You working with him?"

"I... don't know what to... sure, we use... I'll be the first to admit it isn't a good idea to hold onto your real handle if... well, we do change our professional names from time to time so we can maintain our integrity, but..."

Sonny thinks he hears a noise in the hall and springs up from the sofa, fingering silence to his lips with one hand while grabbing his piece with the other. He glides to the door and presses his ear against it, satisfied after several seconds that no one's on the other side, paces back to the sofa like a soldier stalking a shadow, then places his equipment back in its ready location and turns to Mr. Jones.

"Hey, what's going on? Something you didn't tell me?"

"Ask Mr. Smith. He'll fill you in."

"What're you talking about? I don't know anyone by that name."

"Forget the name. He's probably changed it already anyway."

"What's this guy look like?"

"A shadowy blob behind a dusty glass partition in a limo parked in a dark alley under a tree... a rear view of an imposing head... only a brief glimpse of the side of his face. I think it was a male. For a moment I thought I recognized something about him, or her... not sure."

"That's not much to go on. I don't believe I..."

"...the voice seemed distorted. Maybe it was some kinda cyborg. You guys subcontracting robots these days?"

"Funny, funny... though guess that may not be far off."

Sonny gets up and walks around and behind Mr. Jones, giving the back of his head a good inspection. "Some of your words seem..."

"...what're you doing?" Mr. Jones asks as he pivots toward him. "You have a lively imagination. Your headache do that to you? That person isn't anyone I've ever associated with. Maybe we should break and try this again when you get your senses back."

"Sure, tell your people I did my best and I'm sorry but the guy you wanted... well, he was a sleeper and maybe it's best he's still with us because he might be a big help to you guys in the war against..." Sonny's mouth continues to produce half-formed shapes for a few seconds without emitting a sound, then freezes into an oval that obscures most of his ivories, a visual suggesting his mental processes have been momentarily sucked into a black hole. He keeps Mr. Jones in his sights while backstepping to the sofa and his piece like he has eyes in the back of his head. He reaches safety and stretches his arm along the cushion, flexing his hand. Mr. Jones appears not to notice.

"War against what?"

"Every once in a while one slips through my... design, my... you can blame tears in the divine fabric, or flawed celestial advice from... whatever the source is at the moment. I have no control over my moon's movements. I can't rely on my spiritual advisor to keep reshuffling the tarot deck."

"Blame... celestial advice... tarot? What are you..."

"...so give me a break on this one... let me get a handle on this blooper and... I might be able to deal with it myself. Put in a good word for me, will ya?" He flexes his hand again. "Hey, why don't we get all the bosses together and... sorta clear the air and start working together for the same..."

"...what bosses?"

"I need some rest so I'll wait here for your update," he says as he rises from the sofa, motioning Mr. Jones toward the door with his piece. "If it doesn't work out tell 'em I'm ready for 'em."

"Sure," he says on his way out, "ready for... whatever, but why don't you just cool it for a while and I'll get you some help." Sonny shuts the door behind him, secures both of the locks, and pushes a chair flush up against it before returning to the sofa.

Sonny surges to his feet, weapon in hand, at the sound of someone walking in the hallway. After staring at the ceiling for what seemed like hours he finally succumbed to slumber but now he's fairly alert;

he knows where he is and what led to the need to barricade himself inside his place. He learned from his many military missions how to get restful sleep while being sufficiently awake to monitor the activity around him. True, a situation could always surface that would test this ability to have it both ways, but one hasn't yet.

He closed all the blinds earlier so the room is dark except for a faint swatch of light frizzing the zebra plant hanging from the ceiling on the far wall. He shuffles quietly to the door, looking for the knob to turn or the chair to move, but hears only the receding patter of what sounds like a woman's footsteps and retraces his own back to the sofa.

What can he do? Is he doomed to look over his shoulder forever? This isn't the way to live. If he leaves his apartment he's dead. Should he stay with someone else? A pleasant thought but he's burned too many bridges in recent months. This kind of career doesn't exactly help you build a supportive kin network. Maybe he should get out of town for a while, lay low in some desert hovel until things blow over. Who's he trying to fool? They never will completely. But at least he could spend the time training; he has been getting soft lately. Then he could slip back into town and get the upper hand on these bozos.

A few months ago he ran into an old military buddy downtown who said he bought a shack up in the high desert that was miles from normal neighbors but fast becoming a mecca for ex-soldiers like himself who were having a hard time getting work and blending back into civilian life. It turned him off at the time because he was talking some political mumbo-jumbo that he had difficulty grasping and he never joins groups with a lockstep mission. His politics are always practical. Figure the right thing to do in the current circumstances and act accordingly. Sectarians are immoral. Maybe it was time to give up the ghost, snuff these stickmen, and go out in a blaze of glory. Given what he has done and the odds that are stacked against him now, this might be his natural end. He might even become a martyr for those who see the truth like him. But then again, society would be worse off without his contribution. He feels he's a force for good. But there's one thing for sure—he's tired of dealing with second stringers. If he could confront Mr. or Mrs. or Ms. Big face to face he's convinced his talents would be recognized and his actions would begin to produce the best results for everyone involved. He's got to get out of this... prison.

The pain sears through his frontal lobe, twisting his thoughts into a spaghetti of smoldering wires. He inhales the remaining Norcos on the table and wonders if he'll make it through this day. Should he get to a doc? He reaches for his cell and calls Mr. Jones, who starts speaking first.

"I was just going to ring you. I meant to mention that one of the money trails I've been following apparently leads to a new player... someone who might be pulling the strings and owns big chunks of the city. I'll keep..."

"...sure, sure... I hear ya, but I think I need... who's that doc you mentioned that can..."

"...you okay? Knew you needed help. I'll have him contact you right away. Stay with your phone."

Sonny can barely process his words. He's not sure what he asked or what the response was. He can see only wavy white lines set against a red background that now begin to join and then break off into thousands of superfine strings that gather into balls and... finally they all disappear and there's nothing but an azure void that peels away and... he now sees his front door with the chair wedged below the knob but the image splits in two. He shakes his head to fuse them together, but each changes into a different expression of his face, one fearful and the other mordant. He keeps shaking but they remain separate like they're mockingly spying on each other. Then the two join and the entire image disappears, leaving a clear frontal shot of the chair and door. Frustrated, he shakes his head repeatedly but the picture doesn't change. He takes a deep, relaxing breath, elated at the return of his sight and the diminished pain, but wonders how long this will last as his cell lights up with a number he doesn't recognize. He jumps up from the sofa like he expects someone to burst through the door as a jolt of pain to his head sends him back down.

Lying supine for several seconds as the pain fortunately passes, he reflects on why they're calling him. Who are they? He now realizes they wouldn't... it would be out of character for them. It's the doc! It has to be. Seeing there's no message yet, he instantly calls back and gets a woman's panicky voice.

"Thanks... thanks for calling back! Didn't think you would."

"Sure... you the doc? Need some help as soon as possible. It's better now but spent a couple hours..."

"...no, you got the wrong... I'm not a doc. We talked recently at my place over on Clubhouse. Remember?"

"Not... what'd we talk about? How'd you get this number?"

Clara modulates her tone of voice, hoping to keep him on the line.

"About doing a job for our neighborhood improvement committee. We'd already talked on the phone. Met at my condo one afternoon and..."

"I'd remember that for sure." Sonny wonders what sort of crackpot has decided to bother him now. "What's this about?" He eyeballs his phone, hoping to see a call coming in from the doc.

"We referred you for a job. Did they ever contact you about it?"

"You! Are you rubbing it in or... look, lady, why are you contacting me now?"

"Did you complete it?"

"Did I complete it? You gotta be kidding me, lady! You got me that gig and don't know what happened?" His thoughts are becoming clearer—the pain killers have reached their point of maximum efficiency—but he dreads the inevitable drop-off.

"We just passed your name on. You came highly recommended from an acquaintance of ours."

"You're a referral service? No interest in what it was all about?"

"To a point. We're working with other neighbors to get rid of street criminals and other scum that are invading our neighborhoods. But an agency we've been working with hands out the assignments. We're mostly a pressure group that represents homeowners in the city. We go to meetings and..."

"...you mean you don't work directly with Mr. Smith?"

"I'm not familiar with the name? Who's that?"

"He's the contact from your referral."

"Names at the agency aren't reliable... they're always changing them. But whoever's in charge at the moment doesn't matter. There's always someone and he or she has the leeway to execute our intentions.

The agency came well-recommended too. It has been successful in cleaning up many other places."

"You chose the right word, lady... almost got executed by one of your street criminals. What did you get me into? Who is that guy they had me follow? Didn't see how he..."

"...we know about some problem people and spots but not sure which one they targeted for you. The agency does the profiling... the work-ups."

"You had me believing he... now they're probably coming after their payment and... they're not as reasonable-sounding as you, out there enforcing some lawless vendetta with their own authority, executing sentences with limited information and..."

"...why? What happened?"

"I... well, let's leave it at that... not totally sure who you are so..."

"...let's meet on neutral ground... you'll see it's me. I'll call back with the time and place. We'll sort it out. You know how to contact your contact? There are some changes at the agency and we can't reach those in charge."

"I never got a clear look at my contact and dealt with him by phone. Later a woman who met me at the Sidewalk paid me in the back of a limo." Visions of that night, of her and her casual, adventurous mindset toward the grave circumstances he faced at that point rush him and he realizes how absurd the situation is. An actress who's working as a temp for a company that puts out contracts, who has theories about sex and aggression and proper action and... the whole enterprise is run by someone from the entertainment industry, a Mr. Smith, who has full knowledge of his actions and movements. And she lays him in the back seat to boot, supposedly to demo her theory of how an active libido creates a clearer focus. She blew his mind in order to condition him for the job, make him a more efficient operative with the physical confidence to bluster his way toward the goal, but perhaps blew his moral assurance instead. Is this why he failed? She drained him of more than his natural fluids and he missed a beat. So he won the argument but lost the game and now they're going to rub it in, get repayment for the blown job and... possibly vaporize him. Will his body ever be found?

He morosely ponders this state of affairs for several seconds. Then the latent signs of laughter appear. It begins with a suppressed giggle and evolves into a demonic gurgling sound. He busts a gut, the first time he's had a good laugh in weeks. Then the pain returns and he thinks they may not have to off him after all. Now the pain dissipates and he busts another one, but this time it doesn't return.

He stares at the front door, still wary of someone breaking in, but wonders how they could possibly take his blooper seriously given the absurdity of the whole situation. On the other hand, they must certainly see it as a blooper and feel the urgent need to wipe it from the books and... he's being set up! Why else would she call him? Images of this woman caller meld with those of Marci, the former's smiling, plasticized guile and the latter's raw parasitical clawing, both aging seductresses stealing his life force, duping him into a course that deals death. He has an aggressive urge to wipe all this off the record with actions that won't be weakened by his expending his vital fluids. How satisfying it would be to get them before they get him.

His cell flashes again with her number and he realizes he left her in limbo. He hesitates but answers the call.

"What happened? You were saying something about a woman in the back of a limo. Well, you got closer than us. Know how to reach her?"

"Nah, they don't pass out business cards. I'm sure you can find her... them. They're closer to your world than..."

"...yeah but three heads are better than one. I'll bring Cyril. You talked to him briefly on the phone. Let's meet at Figaro's at four-thirty, along the side in the back."

"Not sure I can be there... depends on my doctor's appointment and..."

"...what's wrong? Need some medical help. We'll get you someone right away if you want."

"Think I got it covered... should know in the next half hour or so what to expect. If you don't hear from me I'll be there."

He cuts the call before she can speak, upset with himself for agreeing to meet. Outside Figaro's in the back. He could slip behind them and get it over with. Maybe not a bad move after all. Where's the doc's call? He's thankful his pain hasn't returned as a twinge spreads through his body, more like a mild aftershock compared to his previous ordeal, but enough to make him wonder if he should stop using his head for a while. But how? He tries to imagine his brain cells closing down for a rest but the twinge seems to stimulate them further. Is this the mind's revenge against threatening matters? He needs to relax and meditate but there's no time. Another twinge sends him reeling to the medicine cabinet. Who needs a doc? Most of 'em are quacks anyway. His first aid kit has always done the job. But the cabinet's virtually bare. Has someone ripped him off? He retreats to the sofa and wills regression to a vegetative state with breathing exercises he'd learned in the military, losing consciousness for a few moments. When it returns his head is clear and the pain is mostly gone.

His trusty therapist Ezra will probably have something for him, so why hadn't he contacted him right away? Had he simply come to accept his fate like a beaten warrior? But true warriors never give up. And maybe this latest turn of events will give him more to give Ezra to work with so he can help him get through this. Almost involuntarily, he hits the numbers on his cell.

"Ezra! It's your work in progress... one of them at least. Must've caught you in a lull since you answered right away."

"Yeah, sure... got a little down time. Who's this?"

"Your bro with the iffy date of birth... the smooth hands."

"That's lots a dudes. Can you give me more data?"

"Was just there a few days ago. You invited me to a primal scream therapy group so I could sort things out."

"Oh, sure... right. I apologize bro... got a lot on my mind. Problems with my financial empire. A shake-up you might say."

"Your financial empire? What empire? You mean you stashed away a lot more bucks than you told me about when you were flipping properties?"

"Well, I guess I never talked about it much but... the bucks help me deliver the goods for my clients, give 'em the freedom and happiness they deserve and... but this is all pretty boring stuff for you."

"Not really... always assumed you had to still be involved in the money game on some level since it sounds like you were very successful at it and... looks like I was right. But I'm not sure there are that many deserving clients out there among the street trash anyway, and that seems to be a lot of your clients."

"You included, bro. Just kidding! But the head's like a market. You figure your profit and loss, your supply and demand ratios and such for the psyche. So I'm a natural."

"You mean my head's like a balance sheet... a flow chart?"

"Improving the quality of someone's psyche requires the right capital investment in good energy and feelings so their life can flow profitably."

"Maybe patients can heal themselves if they have enough real capital... your loser clients will become winners and their head issues will go away."

"Well, my altruism only goes so far. But your situation doesn't have much to do with these issues."

"Okay... you got me for now. But let's meet. Some things have happened I have to tell you about... really need help. And I could really use some of your substances."

"Can't right now... am away from the area and not sure when I'll be back in the groove. Clients on hold until I get my house in order." Voices suddenly fill the cyberspace, like Ezra has moved the phone to another area of the place he occupies and left it idle.

"You still there? Ezra, you there?" The only sounds he hears are intercutting conversations. It seems like a few people are arguing about something.

"Sorry bro, caught me in the middle of some family biz. Like I said, gotta attend to my empire but you're in my thoughts and..."

"...my thoughts aren't very clear right now. You left me kinda hangin' last time and the assignment I was considering went bad. This dude..."

"...have any new inputs for me? We can come up with different outputs so you can avoid unforeseen traps and dodge the bad people and obstacles. Shoulda come to the primal scream group. Once ya get all the yeah yeahs and nah nahs out you're the master of your fate. Nothing else will matter out there in the bloody world anymore. Shout it out, even if you choose a bad card. Reshuffle the deck."

"Before or after the screaming?"

"Whatever. Before, during, and after."

"You mean my actions will no longer make me a traitor... new cards will replace old ones?"

"The screaming and choosing are symbiotically related. You..."

"...how do you know when you've arrived at a moment when the right option presents itself ? Maybe you didn't get all the feelings out and..."

"...have to get to an energy flow where you feel you've made the right choices... where your mind is purged of all the impurities and hesitations and hang-ups and..."

"...so it's good to get laid right before then, too?"

"Absolutely. Stew the fluids... purge your libido."

"My energy flow last time did seem... I mean when I was doing the job I had the feeling that I had the wrong subject and was kind of a traitor. I hesitated and the dude surprised me and..."

"...there you go!"

"But a woman got me off right before. Not enough to override the rest?"

"Were you conflicted about it?"

"Wouldn't say that, but it was pretty weird... not very relaxed."

"Maybe it's the way... was it a one-on-one experience?"

"Back seat of a limo on a dark street with one... woman."

"Well, that sounds inviting but... maybe you should do it in a group that screams together in wild abandon. That's what my..."

"...well, I guess I blew it. So if you'd reshuffled the deck last time and I'd picked a different card, then what happened to me might not have?"

"If you'd been fully purged and... a few of the right substances wouldn't have hurt either. By the way, my RV is parked in the lot on the beach just off Rose. My artist buds are watching it while I take care of this unfinished business. You know where my stashes are and... you certainly know how to gain entry. If not, then get in touch with Mimi... she does charts on the boardwalk just down from the Waterfront Café."

"Terrific... thanks! In the meantime I'll get some new info about my time and date of birth and..."

"...we'll get you a new package asap. Also, I'll be meeting with this hot new Sufi from Palmdale right away when I get back into the scene."

Ezra cuts the call without waiting for a response, but Sonny's not sure he has much more to say anyway. His conversational momentum expires with the click and he relishes the wordless hiatus. He expected his head to begin pounding again at any moment during the conversation but it didn't, which only increased his anxiety that the worst was still coming.

But for now his head feels clear and pain-free, like maybe the mere fact of speaking was therapeutic. He reclines on the sofa and falls asleep for several minutes, waking to a desire for clarity. Ezra's words consume him. Reshuffling! If he could only believe he has such a power he might be able to... do what? Will he have to bring the right deck with him at all times and become expert at choosing the right one when necessary?

Ezra's comments are a confidence booster. For a moment he wants to rush out and take care of all his enemies, especially that woman and her cronies. No more of this waiting around. But then he ponders Ezra's advice. If he could successfully purge himself of all impurities and hesitations and hang-ups—and he's certainly not anywhere near that yet—would he be better equipped to make the right choices or... become more indecisive and even unreliable? Will living through a continual purging only muddle his mind? Trying to get the energy to flow in the most efficient way... sure, that's a must for a clear head and... who needs a shrink for that. But won't purging only lead to exhaustion and without energy what will he do—how will he choose? At the end of letting it all hang out, just doing it, are there only mechanical activities without a cause? Lethargy, where nothing of substance matters? Where you feel good but sensitivity and belief disappear, along with ethics?

He wants to feel some pain, the kind that defers full pleasure and... the pain in his head returns as if responding to a secret summons. It's a different pain from before. Constant but muted; a pain that keeps him alert.

Maybe Ezra's off. He knew about his real estate career, though he didn't meet him until much later and he never discussed that period of his life. He thought Ezra had experienced some sort of conversion, a break with his past driven by a change in values. He seemed to care for people, believe in something more meaningful than numbers and deals. Maybe he still does, and he has faith in Ezra regardless since he's helped him a lot, but from his comments he seems to have a secret life larger than real estate. We all have to deal to survive and do things we don't want to do so we can keep our lives moving along. But if he's preoccupied with numbers and deals again now, can he still be reliable? He may be sincere but when you traffic in certain forces do you lose control over your desires and intentions?

A jolt to his head sends a shudder through his body. It doesn't last long, though, and leaves his head momentarily clear and pain-free, his thoughts liquid. But as he awaits another dose his focus shifts away from reasonable reflections about his situation. It's like the pain that streaked through his cells tapped a region of his mind that conjures morbid skepticism, and the thought that Ezra is setting him up along with the others rushes him as the doorbell rings. This validates his suspicions. He stiffens and reaches for his weapon.

The sound of a female voice briefly diverts his attention from conspiracy.

"It's me. Open up."

A friendly acquaintance?

"Hey, killer. You in there?"

He moves to the door, weapon ready, now recognizing who it is and wondering why she's here. They probably sent her to soften him up for the kill. Maybe she's some new kind of urban operative, a hit-woman seductress doing her duty for Mr. Smith. For some reason he'd blocked her out of his mind, separated her from the rest. But now the memories return and he suspects she's central to the cabal, probably in cahoots with Ezra. They're both believers in purging.

He recalls the sensations from the back seat of the limo, the hot streams that challenged his mind. He tried to curb, or at least manage them. The more he agreed to give himself to them the more something fought back. Pleasure fostered an unknown disturbance in his head. It went beyond losing focus. It felt like his firm convictions were going limp. And as his body palpitated his thoughts seemed to vaporize. When he came he felt like he'd lost something.

"Who is it?"

"You know who I am. I charged up your body and... paid you for your good deeds."

"Why are you here?"

"What are you afraid of ? We're in the same..."

"...who's with you?" he asks, suspecting it's Marci.

"Nobody. Need to talk. Been lots a changes and you need to know what they are."

He unlatches the door carefully from the side while cocking his weapon and peeks through the widening slit, not sure if he should give her entry. He opens the door a little wider to see if anyone else is with her and motions her in. She looks different from before. Is it the light? Had she been wearing a disguise?

"What's so urgent? *They* send you?" He returns to his protected roost on the sofa, keeping her at a distance as she slinks into the recliner on the other side of the room and lounges back, her legs spread apart. He lays the weapon down within easy reach of his stiffened arm, fighting off temptation.

"They? There's no..."

"...tell 'em I did my best and will make it up."

He does a double take at this first face-off. She's dressed a lot differently than before and is wearing no makeup. It's like she just left the office at the end of the day. Like her boss, maybe she's a master ventriloquist. He wonders if she has a weapon.

"Your best what? To whom?"

"Your boss, Mr. Smith. He gave me an assignment... remember?"

"Well, he's no longer in the picture and... don't have any details about your assignment because..." She crosses her legs while retrieving her makeup paraphernalia.

"Why? I thought you... from our conversation it sounded like you were part of the planning."

"Yeah, I was but... well, the monitors for your case sort of went on strike and... that's what I'm trying to tell you, the situation's changed. There's been a communication breakdown. Mr. Big disappeared after a couple of big dudes with accents came to the office asking tough questions that I didn't understand. It seems somebody else or some company took over the business and the paychecks stopped. I got an interview later through my agency... a chance for a role in this flick they're making at a ranch out in the valley. But I was on my way out anyway... memos were a bummer. Tired of memorizing words that don't make sense and disguising my voice. I'm an actress but I deserve better roles than that!"

"You're an actress, all right... had *me* fooled." He stares at her, not sure what to say as her makeup metamorphosis provides more proof of her skills. She seems ready to perform another role.

He looks at her skeptically. "Paychecks, roles, business decisions, strikes... how can this be? You mean no one's in charge?"

"That's the world of biz... I've been through it before. Nothing to get worried about. The company will get reconstituted or whatever. Sounds like maybe there's gonna be a merger or something. Don't know anything about that stuff."

"But I thought this company was above all that... it was about getting the right things done and using the right people with the right ideas to make them happen."

"These ideals will probably survive and get executed with other good people soon."

"That word again. I almost got executed by some dude I was following."

"The one you were assigned to... watch?"

"Yes. He caught me off guard and gave me a nasty rap on my head that... the pain keeps coming back."

"You look okay... wouldn't worry about it. You just need a good massage." She gets up from the recliner and starts to step toward him as he grabs his weapon, then stops in her tracks.

"Whoa, killer! What you been smokin'? We're mates."

"Maybe we are... maybe. I can't be too careful since... a massage sounds great but also gotta get to my therapist's place for some meds... somebody out there is gonna want their bread back for this botched job and will probably want to cancel any trace of it too... maybe they'll even want me to redo it. All the players aren't going away. That's not the way this racket works. Plus the dude I followed... don't think he was someone who shoulda... well, he wasn't the dude I expected."

"If he was targeted then that's enough... assignments are assignments. Someone with the know-how makes a call and it's finished. Another person would do it anyway so you're off the hook.

Your role has no meaning."

"But if those above us are dealing with this other stuff, how can they do the right thing for..."

"...the two have nothing to do with each other. All businesses have to be in good shape so they can deliver services. Come on, stop talking silly. Let me see your killer weapon!"

He instantly thinks of Ezra and pulls back, leaving her hand suspended. Does she know him? Are they partners? He wants to tell her that he thinks the guy he followed might have been the wrong one... but apparently she doesn't know what his assignment was. Is she naïve or heartless? It probably doesn't matter at this point anyway but... something's not right about this company. Mr. Smith's quirks in the limo begin to make sense. She's just a victim like him.

"They... someone knows where I live and... this situation will never get resolved unless I..."

"...we can go to my place. I'm staying with this dude but he won't mind."

"Don't they know where you live?"

"No one knows... made sure of that! Soon I wanna try and find some of the operatives who vanished. They're good people and... don't want them to start freelancing without knowing what happened. They might try to get revenge too. Grabbed a few files from the office to make some sense of all this."

A streak of pain sears his right lobe and he pulls her hand toward him.

Sonny's eyes twitch twice in rapid succession and open to a swatch of wall framed by Marci's legs, the canted angle disorienting him. He tries to ease his body from under them without waking her, but as his left foot drops from the sofa to the floor she pincers him back into position.

"You're not gonna get away from me that easy... c'mere, killer," she says groggily while reaching for his head.

"I can't... got a meeting at Figaro's with the woman who set me up with that gig. I'm worried. It's a loose end. I should clear that up... get them off my back now or I may regret it later."

"What woman?"

"You don't remember? She's the one who sent me to you... how could you forget?"

"We have... or I should say *had* a lot a clients so it's easy, plus we actively cancel as many paper trails as we can without compromising our security. Anyway, that's what I was told to say. Names clog up the system. I was told to say that too. So you can imagine that I haven't spent much time memorizing them."

"Then it could be worse. If they're cut off they might feel betrayed and take revenge... it's blowback from the botched job. I might not ever get away from that if I don't act."

"Not likely those people will do that. As I said, the freelancers might, though not against us. They might follow the wrong people if they didn't get their final instructions but were paid. I'm gonna try and reach a few whose cases I know to give them the heads up."

"The woman also asked me how to reach you guys."

"Hope you didn't tell her."

"Didn't know how... my only contact with you was by pay phone."

"Forget that too."

"Let's both go and meet her... I'll feel much safer."

"Let's avoid her and her friends... get away from here. Nothing to be gained from it. They'll be contacted when the company gets it together. You're making too much of this. They don't know how to reach you, right?"

"No... well, I'm not sure. And when I'm not sure I have to make sure, otherwise you pay."

"You're into final solutions, aren't you, killer?"

"Why do you... you have my file?"

"Had a peek at it then but don't think it still exists. I know you're a hero and you'll get your rewards someday. And you're a born actor. You can get passionate about your assignments. Maybe I can get you into this film."

"What film?"

"The one I told you about earlier. It's an erotic, new wave western... whatever that is. They're shooting it next weekend at a ranch out in the valley. You'd be perfect for..."

"...how do you know? Wouldn't I need a screen test?"

"That look you have. I've been around for a while... consider me a talent scout. You look like nothing matters but everything does. Maybe it's time you explored a different career."

"What would I have to do? I don't..."

"...be yourself. You already seem to be acting some good parts. Who's that guy... Steven somebody? The undercover agent that kills with his..."

"...there you go again with that killer stuff!"

Could she be setting him up? Maybe she's recording their conversations, filming them together with some hidden device to get him to reveal information. It makes perfect sense. She was sent by Mr. Big to clear up the loose ends... clear away all the contractual debris littering the streets with her physical talents. Part-time student, itinerant actress, shrink, confidant, nurse making house calls. It's too good to be true. Why didn't he see it earlier? She seems too confident and... has too many ready answers. He has to admit she's good for him now though. He feels more relaxed. And the pain hasn't returned since she arrived. But that's suspicious too. Did she drug him after she serviced him... after he dozed off ? The more fluids she takes out of him the more confused he gets. She might be some kind of siren sucking the life out of him. All that crap about purging his libido to condition himself to be the most efficient warrior. He's losing focus... his ability to make clear moral distinctions.

He often got erections from planning and performing his actions, but only if he was convinced they were correct ones and he'd abstained. He saved his wargasms for afterward. It has to be a setup. They knew this libido crap was just a way to entrap him. His reduced level of vital fluids caused his conscience to equivocate and distracted him just enough to make him fail. They probably had a change of plans and decided he was to be hit by the perp and not the other way around. Why is she so against him meeting that woman? She's probably afraid he'll find out too much about their operation.

"Hey, snap out of it!" She nudges him gracefully but can't break the trance and slips her hands around his thighs. "Wake up, killer!" The elevated sonority of her missive rustles him and she clasps his limp member with both hands like she's trying to firm up a willowy cactus for planting in the loose soil. As she stiffens her creation with the tip of her tongue he rolls onto the floor like he's evading a strike from an unknown enemy. The shadows configure her face in a giddy question mark, blanking the left side of her succulent oval and suggesting a line dangling below from the effect of her dimpled chin.

"No more... I gotta get it together."

"You sure do!" Her lips flatten to a slit of baffled ivory that repels him. She seems alien to him... an intruder in his space. She suddenly effervesces a pearly string of clarity. "But you're going about it in the wrong way, sweetie. You need to trust the people who can guide you to the promised land."

"If they're not the right ones you end up with broken promises and a ticket to the underworld."

"But if you don't take the plunge and give it your best shot you end up in limbo or a place like this, always worried about what's gonna happen!"

"Yeah, I get your drift but... I gotta get cleaned up and get ready for the day." He gets up from the floor onto his haunches and springs upright into a stiffening drill posture, turning toward her with a look that says he has everything under control before limping off to the bathroom.

"You should wash some of that confusion off while you're in there... get a good drench."

He releases the water and glares at the showerhead in anticipation of relief, waiting for the drops to pick up their pace, and imagines himself under a forest canopy dodging raindrops, his movements resembling a tribal dance. He watches the drops descend toward his face and freeze, suspended before him. Then they melt and increase in number, drenching him in blood that expands into a pool from which he tries to escape.

Marci rises to follow him into the bathroom but abruptly stops as she hears the water running and returns to the sofa. What can I do to convince him I have his best interests in mind? She looks around and tries to form a clear picture of who he is from his surroundings when she notices the butt of a gun exposed from under a pillow and flashes a private, nervous grin. It excites her to know that it was that close when she was draining his fluids. But what if she had gone too far, reduced him to a babbling idiot for a few minutes, which she knows she can do if the conditions are right? She senses he could be dangerous and this excites her, but could he be aggressive toward her? She doesn't know him very well but he's acting very strange. Should she fear for her life? What will it take to channel his aggression and turn him into an uninhibited, loving person? She needs a different pose.

In the meantime, though, they've got to get out of here. She peruses the files in her bag and decides she'll make a few calls from her place and try to straighten out as many messes as she can. And then what? Up to that filming site for sure, but what after that? Maybe they should both get as far away from this city as possible. There's little that can be done here now. They're both out of their element—hyper-heated beings in search of the right roles that will probably never come in this society they find themselves in. If she can figure the right button to push she could get him to escape with her to the high desert and lose themselves among the lizards, snakes, and coyotes. Maybe carve out a cave in the buttes.

The water stops running and her fantasy dissolves. Hopefully the soak has mellowed him and they can make some constructive plans. She edges along the sofa and smothers the cold steel with her twitching pillows. The cold sensation diminishes but its shape nests awkwardly under her right buttocks and she wiggles to her right, wedging it comfortably into the crease. Wondering what's taking him so long she glances toward the bathroom, shifting her torso ever so slightly, but the movement back to the original position rouses a vexing emotion, like a conscious prosthesis has begun to stroke her. In her titillation she realizes it could possibly discharge and she freezes as a robed Sonny appears in her bleary line of sight. He witnesses a face morphing from pained rapture to fear and looks around the room.

"Did I interrupt you? Were you meditating?"

"No... well sorta. Just daydreaming a little, I guess." She speaks slower than usual, and at a higher octave. "It took you so long. What were you doing in there? Getting clean for me? Don't worry, I'm not gonna steal any more of your fluids."

"Good. Let me rest up a bit and replenish 'em." He notices that she's sitting upright and stiff. "You okay?"

"Sure. But could you reach between my legs and carefully remove your..."

"...my what?"

"Your weapon... what you deliver.... substances with."

"You mean my..."

"...yeah, that's what I mean! I had to have something to replace you. If you hadn't come when you did I might have had the deadliest orgasm of my life." He stares at her speechless. What's going on in this woman's head?

"It was an accident, just happened to sit on it... trying to hide it so I could get your mind on something more positive."

He inches toward her with a look of anxious

desperation, like he's preparing to defuse a time bomb.

"Relax... it's not that likely to go off," she says.

"That depends on what your muscles have been up to... if you released the safety then..."

"...we can play roulette. That's your game too, isn't it? It can fine-tune your senses, your brain..."

"...and finish your existence. I'm only prepared to gamble when the stakes are credible and I'm certain that it's the right... course." He slides his hand slowly under her crotch, his wiggling fingers focused.

"We don't always know what that is so we have to take chances... we discover options when we push to the edge. That's what we do in acting classes." Her face has a rosy glow.

"If we know where to stop and... don't fall off." He finds a warm crease of steel and skin but pulls his hand back as she jerks her left leg. "Stay still... just a bit more."

She snorts a grin. "This is a new experience for me. I've never been aroused by a foreign object before."

He slips his fingers into the moistening cavity and carefully removes the piece, holding it in his hand while glaring at her. She appears relieved but frustrated.

"It looks like you're a survivor." He passes the metal over the sofa's surface to make it shiny and dry.

"Was it loaded?"

"It's always loaded."

"You're not gonna put it back in are you?"

"I'm gonna put it where I can get it quick and where it doesn't cause any more trouble. I gotta get crackin'... take care of business. I'm not gonna wait here for them to come after me."

"I'm not so sure there is a them... at least not

anymore. Whoever had it in for you—if they did—has probably already forgotten you."

"In this business you never forget."

"The business has changed."

"If no one's minding the store and... the company's in chaos like you say, then the best approach might be to step in and take charge. Offense is the best defense. Chaos breeds the conditions that encourage the gifted to fulfill their potential and lead the masses. Ever read Carlyle?"

"Does he write scripts?"

"No, no... never mind. You said it yourself... people are always being replaced. I could run an organization and... shape a better society if I could get hold of the right people."

What's he talking about, she wonders. What happened to him in the shower? Maybe she should put some fluids into *his* body. "How about heading to my place and... then off to the high desert. Got some..."

"...your place sounds okay but no desert for me now. Can you help me get in touch with those employees that disappeared? You said you had files."

"I got 'em, but... what can they do for you now?"

"They can help me figure out the operation... what it was like... and maybe lead me to Mr. Smith?"

"Why do you need him?"

"He'll have the information I need to get me to the source... the anonymous puppet master who pulls the strings from an unknown location... the one responsible for letting this scene get out of control."

"He got his instructions like you and probably never had any personal contact with anyone. I don't think he cared much anyway. As long as he got his check he was pretty content."

"Like most of us but... there must be some clues, a trail of some kind that leads to the source."

"I wouldn't count on it."

"I got a nose for sniffing these things out... I can make people talk."

"You should use your talents in a more productive way."

"Don't you support me?" He looks her directly in the eye but she flinches and turns away sharply.

"Yes, but... well, I'm not all that sure what you're doing. You may be getting into something you know nothing about and... you might set events in motion that destroy you. Nobody wins at playing the revenge game."

"I just wanna be ready for anyone who comes after me and... be the one who replaces this free enterprise approach to justice with a commitment to truth. No more corporations... only associations of people motivated by belief in something greater than profits. Balancing debits and credits will never lead to the fairest measures. We need something like what they have in the Mideast but on a smaller scale and more accountable... a caliphate that cares."

She's looking him directly in the eye now, unsure how to respond. If she can quickly get him to a different scene, maybe he'll come out of it.

"There's no such thing as perfect justice. You've got some corny idea of morality that's out of date. It's not real. Profit's the only motivator of people now. That's what they understand... not wacko religious nonsense. That always leads to the death of innocent victims. You gonna be the priest who decides for everyone else? Mr. Smith said if you just stay focused on the bottom line everything works out like it should.

The market is the best solution to right and wrong. It automatically adjusts and takes care of all glitches. Some sort of checks and balances protects us from mistakes."

"They didn't protect his job."

"They probably sent him to a better one... and we're all better off now. The market intervened and corrected the situation."

"With all those unpaid operators wandering the streets looking for..."

"...he would say we're in a period of adjustment now and..."

"...innocent victims are being sacrificed."

"Let's just go play house... get away from here. Why are you so obsessed with all this?"

"Get away from here for sure but..." A numbing sensation at the base of his skull blocks his thought processes and gradually suffuses through his brain as though a gas pellet has released a substance that makes the objects in the room appear more vibrant and fluid. But the details are missing. He looks at her but sees only highlights. The inside of his head now becomes a pinball machine with spheres careening off his skull in a serpentine geometry. She pulls him down onto the sofa and works his shoulders but he springs up and paces the room, holding his head. He pivots toward her.

"I feel like some spirit has entered my body. It's enlightening in a strange way but then it suddenly seems like my head is going to fall off. I'm... okay now. I... can see better, think more clearly."

"For how long? This isn't normal. You need a doc or maybe a good massage."

"Need some meds... my shrink has the substances that'll work." He steps to the coffee table and retrieves his piece, inspecting it carefully before securing it. "I'm otta here. Give me your number and I'll call you later when I'm done."

"I'll call you and give you the address where I'll be."

"Afraid I'll expose you?"

"Expose me? I don't have..."

"...you're covering your tracks just like..."

"...no, no... been staying a couple places and I get too many sleazy calls as it is and wanna keep my number as secret as possible."

"Think I would give it out?"

"Not now but... you could change your mind."

What did Ezra say that woman's name was who could get him into his RV? Miriam? Melanie? Melina? Sonny is sitting in the pagoda off Dudley gawking through the branches of a eucalyptus at seagulls dive-bombing into the water. He could get in easily enough, as Ezra suggested, but he doesn't want to draw attention to himself, especially now. He would've written the name down but he got lost in their conversation.

The pain hasn't returned but he's afraid it will eventually and wants to be prepared. He begins to muse about Ezra's comments on his astrological chart, that it wasn't reliable because of his faulty birth data, and wonders if it'll matter. It seems events are moving awfully fast and he'll have to make some tough choices soon. No time for reflection and advice.

The convergence of circumstances will give him a therapeutic release or... lead to his demise. Correct action will expose the issues that need to be addressed and present their solutions at the same time. The heat of decision-making can eliminate doubts and demons.

A faulty chart on the other... charts! That's it.

He said she did charts on the boardwalk. But where? If he knew where, he could probably pick her out. He decides to stroll along the boardwalk and see if the carnival gels his memory. He saunters into the South Beach Café to get a coffee and takes a seat along the wall to wait for the line to shorten when his eyes become glued to the sign in the corner with the café's name on it. It's like the lettering is a complex syntactical phrase that's flashing from some subliminal storehouse, demanding to be deciphered. South Beach! South Beach! South Beach! Miami. Mimi! Sure. Mimi who does charts down from the Waterfront Cafe. All that headwork and not even a twinge of pain... maybe he doesn't need Ezra after all.

He bolts from the café onto the boardwalk but sees no one who appears to be doing charts on this side of the Waterfront, only a few hundred feet away. Noticing there are merely a few tables remaining below the South Beach, he realizes that most of the mindwares have likely been stored in the memories of the healing faithful for another day. They know how threatening the strip can suddenly become at the edge of twilight.

A shrill, trebly voice pierces the din. "Gail, you got my jacket in your backpack?" Sonny turns and sees a shadowed frame sauntering across the boardwalk to the parking lot bordering the strand where several people are loading items into RVs and other vehicles. Gail's answer is drowned out by the metal-on-pavement roar of passing skaters, but the questioner's beeline to the lot has the effect of urging him toward them. She might be Mimi or they might know where she is.

He makes it to within about ten feet and stops, leaning against a palm tree to take in the scene. It seems to be a lively group of artists who know each other well and whose dress, mannerisms, and street cant evoke the sort of lifestyle that Ezra cultivates. A super-sized boom box is perched on the tailgate of a rusted-out woody. A male in his forties walks over and replaces the sitar salve with heavy-metal Slayer tonic, giving the volume knob an extra turn for good measure. The jolt of the decibels seems to speed up the work effort, but draws poison darts from amblers along the east side of the boardwalk.

Paintings, political posters, tees, containers of food, and books are finding their daily niches. The woman who crossed the boardwalk is putting a table, chair, and box of materials into an RV that looks familiar. Since she's working separately from the rest, he decides to swing around them and grab her attention.

"Get away... what are you doing here? You don't belong here." The woman jerks her body away from him and reaches for a club lying inside the door of the RV.

"Peace! Just wanna get some information. I'm not gonna bother you." Sonny thinks he recognizes her from somewhere, though the lighting is not very cooperative. "I'm looking for Mimi. Know where I can find her?"

"Why do you want her?"

"You know her then?"

"Who sent you? Who gave you my name?" Her voice elevates and the others drop their items and proceed to encircle them. He peruses their faces—dropout types untested in the jungle of actual confrontation—as pain streaks across his right lobe. She notices the wince and shutters his facial expression, the infirmity giving her even more of a reason to repel him. He's not even looking directly at her, and each eye seems focused on a different object, conjuring the presence of someone who's an imminent threat, perhaps ready to do violence against her.

"Ezra," he says, his eyes now in sync. "He has been helping me and said to contact you about getting something I need in his RV while he's away."

"He never said anything to us," Mimi responds, trying to imagine what sort of bond could exist between the two. "In fact, he hasn't talked to us for some time. He's unreachable." Before she completes the sentence, she's beginning to sense that he at least loosely resembles the sort of client Ezra attracts.

"He's AWOL," interjects a male in his forties who appears ready to spring at Sonny at the slightest provocation. "Left us in the lurch."

"Maybe he didn't think he needed to mention it... maybe he's working through some personal issues like we all have to once in a while, or... at a conference to bone up..."

"...he needs lotsa conferences. Our mate Libraham's in the county psych ward. Got some screwball advice and bad chemicals from our broker."

"No one's perfect. I'll accept full responsibility. It's not your problem. Just need to get in there for a bit. You can watch me... won't take long."

"You look like you need something!" adds a bespectacled male in his twenties who looks like a cross between Woody Allen and Allen Ginsberg. "Maybe he gave you a bad batch of stuff too."

"Nah, he's been straight with me... understands the minds of the needy. I just need some pills. He's given them to me before. Got a headache. Where's his RV?" He shifts his weight toward Woody Allen Ginsberg just enough to suggest he means business and glances stealthily at the others.

"This is it," Mimi says, sensing a refusal to answer might bring unwanted trouble from a psycho. "I... we've been taking care of it for him. If he treated you before why didn't you know it was his?"

"Thought it looked familiar. I'm never in my best shape when I meet him there."

"Since he left we've had lots of strangers come around asking about him, and asking about us... probably your friends."

"Like I said, just need to get in his RV and I'm gone. Got no friends that would be coming around here."

"They're kinda like you, though. Some even threatened us with violence so we got weapons to defend ourselves. We're ready for you." Sonny thrives on one-upmanship and meets her gaze with a surprising brashness, making sure she and the others see the bulge in his pocket by shifting his posture.

"You can't get us all," says Woody Allen Ginsberg as he fades to the fringe waving his cell above his head.

"Look, I just want to get something inside."

"Okay... okay. Tell us what the inside looks like then," says Mimi.

"Lots of books stacked up all over the place... poster of Megadeth... a..."

"...okay. We didn't start getting these strangers coming round until Ezra split... so we're not sure what's going on and wanna be careful. They don't explain very much. They're very evasive. Since he hasn't kept in touch with us, maybe there's an issue we don't know about and he sent them himself... trying to intimidate us. But that doesn't seem like him. At least not the old Ezra. Or maybe these strangers want to do him harm and if that's so then we certainly don't wanna let that happen. Though he does owe us money... not like him."

"Don't know anything about that. When I talked to him before he left he did seem worried... like he wasn't his usual self. There were some people with him who kept interrupting our conversation and it seemed there was lots of arguing in the background."

"Sounds like he gave out more bad advice," says the male in his forties. "Therapists don't usually get aggressive with each other."

"Who knows what's going on... let's wait it out," adds Mimi. "Ezra's done some crazy things before."

Sonny certainly agrees with Mimi and wants to support Ezra but hesitates, hoping to get to the coda with a brief glance at her and then the others, but their looks only mirror their words. He processes these slants on Ezra and wonders if there's more going on than he thought. "Well, haven't we all. I just need a few minutes to get what I came for and I'll be off."

"Go ahead... holler if you need any help," says Mimi in a tone of cooperation that doesn't quite conceal her suspicions.

Sonny recognizes the inside of the RV though someone has clearly cleaned it up some and repositioned many of the books. Did Ezra actually read these books, he wonders, while slipping into the bathroom. He recalls the session when Ezra overwhelmed him with different versions of shrink advice after he opened up about his problems to what seemed like deaf ears. But then again, the gist of that session has proven to be more or less true. It alerted him to forces that are trying to alter his course, even turn him into a traitor. Somehow, Ezra always seemed to get it right enough.

He opens the medicine cabinet to an oversqueezed tube of toothpaste and a capless deodorant. The shock gives his left lobe a jolt and erases the positive picture of Ezra from his memory. He flashes on a hooded figure hanging from the rafters in a large warehouse and closes his eyes. When he reopens them he sees only himself in the mirror and pulls back but has difficulty detaching from his image.

Teetering into the living room, he looks around frantically for places to search and begins tossing everything that's unattached until he realizes the futility of his actions and collapses on the sofa. Think! Where would Ezra hide the goods? It must be in a logical place or he wouldn't have told him to come and get them without specific directions. Behind the books! He recalls once when they were listening to music that Ezra pulled two volumes off the shelf and reached for something behind the vacated space, though he can't remember where. He looks behind every book, under the rugs, and behind every object and piece of furniture in the vehicle but finds no hiding places.

Finally, he inspects the desk in the corner. The top has been completely cleared off except for a book on finance and an empty urn with figures on it that make no sense to him. He feels underneath and behind it but finds nothing. The drawer appears to be locked but releases after a few firm pulls. It contains a small notebook, several pieces of scrap paper, and a calendar with dates circled, some of which have attached balloons with commentary. He can't decipher it but the writing on a few scraps is more legible, mostly to-do lists, reminders of errands and deadlines. He finds a key under the pile and pockets it. Flipping through the notebook he sees mostly blank pages, but one near the end has a list of names with arrows linking several of them together along with a few phone numbers. These are also not very clear, but two of the names appear to be Mr. Smith and Mr. Jones.

"Find what you were looking for yet?" Mimi bellows.

"Not... just about," he responds. "Give me a couple more minutes."

He examines the names but the hieroglyphics around them are confusing and they're placed next to each other on the page, linked by squiggly lines. His focus begins to flag and he doesn't want Mimi or any of her friends to come in after him so he secures the notebook, suspecting that Ezra won't soon be returning for it anyway, and takes one more pass through the RV like he's leaving his own lodgings for the last time.

"Get your stash?"

"Well, yeah... got what I need for now. Thanks and... sorry for the scare. I can see you folks are in Ezra's circle."

"Hope we still are. If we don't hear from him pretty..."

"...here's some cash to keep you going... Ezra's good for it I'm sure." Sonny pulls a wad of bills from his pocket and peels back several, crushing them into a ball and pressing it firmly in Mimi's palm with his right hand against his left on the bottom, holding them for a few seconds in a gesture of sympathy.

"And we almost called 911 on you!" exclaims Woody Allen Ginsberg.

"You wanna be our bodyguard?" asks Mimi. "You seem like you could take care of..."

"...gotta take care of some personal business.

Don't really get involved in that kinda work. If you keep getting bothered just grab some muscle along the beach."

He turns abruptly away and strides toward the boardwalk, eager to examine the notebook though he wishes he could linger a while longer. What is it about these people? They're trying to survive on the beach, victims of some fantasy about living a better life with less. Where do they get that? What's the point? Like monks in a cloister. He feels sort of sorry for them and wonders why. Maybe because Ezra did them bad. But maybe Ezra has also done him bad. Why did he say there would be meds in his RV when there weren't any? Is Ezra the traitor? No, they're messin' with him! Mimi must have found the stash when she was cleaning the place up and they played him to protect themselves. He should go back and take care of business ... straighten all this out. What's he gonna do if the headaches return? He turns around as he reaches the pagoda to get another glimpse of them but they've vanished. Inside the RV? Gone down to the water? Maybe he'll come back later.

Luckily the Bistro is not very crowded and he grabs a corner table that's fairly well lit so he can do his best to make out the writing in the notebook. Why does Ezra have this list in the first place? He doesn't recognize any of the names in it except Mr. Jones and Mr. Smith. Are they the same two people he knows by these names? But who can believe in a name these days, anyway, and these are pretty transparent. Too transparent. They're corny aliases that no serious person would use unless they know no one would believe them and don't care. The names aren't that important. The important part is that everyone accepts that they're going about their business. Is

Ezra involved with the same company? Are these the names of other contractors? What do these lines mean that connect each name? There must be a logical explanation for this list. It could be something one of Ezra's clients left behind, or... the property of one of these losers. They're all involved in this somehow and that's why they've been getting those threats. Ezra wouldn't have ever left this behind. What really disturbs him now is that he suspected earlier that Mr. Smith and Mr. Jones were the same person and here they are. If this is Ezra's doing then he might not be the friend he thought he had. Should he put the notebook back until he knows for sure what's going on? He has to confront Mr. Jones. He'll get the truth out of him one way or the other. Then he'll get up to the high desert and stay with his buddy until things blow over. Does he dare go back to his place for his stuff?

"I need to talk to you right away," Sonny yawps into his cell while footing it down the west side of Speedway, closely monitoring the traffic flow to his left. "Call me back as soon as you..."

"...where you at?" gushes the actual Mr. Jones, like he's been feverishly trying to reach him.

"I'm... out playing detective. Developing some new skills I can use when the..."

"...what do you mean? Why aren't you at your place?"

"How'd you know I wasn't at my place?"

"You... you just said so."

"I'm not now but..."

"...just assumed you had been gone for a while."

"We need to meet. Where's your place?"

"Not here."

"Why? Can I have your address?"

"I can't give..."

"...why? What's the big secret?"

"No secret, just that I gotta stay incognito in... my position... at least right now."

"But my place is like an open house, huh? You guys play your games and we pay for it."

"What're you talking about? Have those headaches of yours caused permanent damage?"

"Not yet. In fact, it seems like I'm seeing better than ever since that botched assignment. But you knew about that, didn't you? Saw your name on a list. Know Ezra?"

"What... list? Assignment? Don't know... who's that? Look, you seem to be losing it. Just tell me where you are and we'll... I'll... come and meet you."

"Not my place. I'm gonna get some stuff there and leave right away."

"We don't need much time... that'll work."

"Okay, but I'll be ready for you. Thirty minutes." Sonny cuts the call.

"Ready for what?"

Sonny hustles down Speedway and crosses between two cars near Thornton, continuing on to the alley behind it, and treads the remaining few blocks to his pad to prepare for his visitor. As he approaches the building a late model maroon Mercedes creeps past him as if the driver is looking for an address. It slows to a stop at the end of the block and abruptly turns right. The car looks familiar, though its tinted windows prevent a look inside.

Sonny pivots and retraces his steps away from the building. When he reaches the end of the block he decides to retrieve his car on Main and park it in an available space across the street from his apartment for a quick getaway, but when he turns onto his street another car slips into the space. He creeps parallel to it for a glimpse but doesn't recognize the driver. He pulls into the alley and parks illegally, giving him a clear vantage of his building across the way.

Yes, Mr. Jones, I'm ready. Where are you? The traffic picks up slightly—more frantic seekers of the vanishing parking spaces. A woman in her forties enters his building but exits a few minutes later and gazes at the top floor, sashaying down the block at the sound of a car entering the street. He hasn't seen her around. Another neighborhood gadfly? Why does he live in a building without a security door?

He checks his cell and wonders if he should call Marci. A street character hobbles by oblivious to the world and stops abruptly, continues on for a few steps, and stops again ten feet or so in front of him, teetering like he's fighting to stay vertical in the final throes of inebriation. Sonny waves him away but he misreads the signal and begins to approach the car. Sonny again waves for him to move on, this time becoming more forcibly graphic. The guy steps back in apparent disappointment, flailing his arms to keep from falling, but once he regains his balance orchestrates his spasms in Sonny's direction. *Does he think I'm beckoning him over?* The guy stops again quickly as if he might have gotten the point this time, then proceeds to dance around in front of the car, bobbing and weaving in a complex series of unlikely angles. Sonny wants to get out and shoo this eyesore away but instead finds himself lost in the choreography, wondering why the guy doesn't fall.

A few moments later the character hobbles slowly toward the driver's side of the car. Sonny keeps his cool but as he comes closer it seems this guy is a woman. He lifts his body to get out and get rid of her but she's at the window now, ogling him.

"Get otta here! Go away!" She remains fixated on him like a demented mannequin with lifelike eye-slits. *Why doesn't he just wipe her out?*

As he ponders this, the passenger door opens and a pair of hands grabs his shoulder in a flash, pulling him across the seat and out the door into the alley where another pair raps him in the mouth. They drag him behind the car, frisk him, and pummel him unconscious. Then they lift his immobilized frame and drop it into the dumpster a few feet further down the alley. His still-breathing body lies spread-eagled atop the previous day's refuse spilling out of torn garbage bags, random streaks of light from a nearby streetlamp exposing a multi-colored collage emitting whimsical fragrances which, if ingested imaginatively, might embalm the spirit. A jagged trail of crushed, coffee ground-speckled eggshells leads from his right lobe down along his outstretched arm like an arrow pointing to his open palm where a cell flashes and then speaks.

"Hey killer! Let's meet in half an hour and plan our escape to... the high desert. Got a friend who'll let us stay there awhile and... you might find some of your family out there and never wanna leave! Got some panicky messages from employees looking for help with their assignments and... paychecks. They'll never find us up "

A partially decomposed pigeon carcass lies near his hand, staring at the cell with bottomless black holes as a revving motorcycle drowns the voice.

FROM THE RUINS OF LLANO DEL RIO

It has been one year since a few hundred Venice citizens occupied a large piece of land with three abandoned warehouses, one of several fallow patches created by the recent recession. This property had remained in limbo after foreclosure because the players were arrested for money laundering, forcing the city to hold it until the issues were resolved.

At first there was fierce resistance to the occupation from the city's powerful and propertied, but as the community grew the mayor was pressured to protect it. It had become a magnet for the homeless population, which had burgeoned since the recession, but also for many who sought something other than a rat race of high rents and a stifling consumerism.

An independent community prospered that was devoted to diversity and equality. It was guided by a core of activists who had survived in the city for several years, with added support from part-time recruits committed to the cause. Their avowed goal was to produce a fully democratic city-state where everyone had a meaningful voice in its affairs, and they proceeded to create the conditions for the flowering of universal literacy. This meant more than upgrading the members' skills. It meant educating them in the desire to discover the truth in the here and now, and especially how to treateach other fairly and bond in a way that encouraged group loyalty without denying personal freedom. A society that was free and continually approaching perfection could not exist without citizens committed to perpetual improvement. Therapy was the key, especially advances in hypnotherapy and the use of a non-addictive, mind-expanding drug developed by Krassly, a local alchemist. It imbued uncluttered reality with the desire for collective sharing through physical contact.

The one-year anniversary arrived on a Sunday, appropriately since it took on the tenor of a religious holiday from the start, though denomination-free and absent the icons and gestures of otherworldly devotion. In place of prostrating themselves before the Beyond and praying to abstractions, they're demoing the spiritual rapture of physical communion with their fellow beings. The spirit is not separate from the body. After working to craft a perfecting society for fifty-two Sundays and banishing zealotry, these Zarathustras and Zarathustresses find themselves at rest in performance and song. If a deity were looking at them from above, he, she, or it would see some 1500 citizens self-choreographing a satyr play with multiple simultaneous scenes, writhing in reciprocating clusters of passion.

A few of the organizers surface from the clusters intermittently to observe the progress of the proceedings. Todd ambles near the perimeter in the southwest corner, very pleased with the course of events. He gazes through the opening in the fence at the outside world, expecting to see a crowd of spectators amassing. The decision to leave the camp virtually open to the surrounding area was unanimous, though not without some debate. Blending their trusty guardians into the gathering seemed at first a bad idea, but the others convinced him that their new citizen policing force was ready for the task. He sees only a smattering of passersby on the street some hundred feet away. A woman off in the distance appears to be looking in his direction. He waves at her and she waves back, possibly taking his acknowledgment as an invitation to approach the camp. Todd wonders if the outside world has forgotten them. Or maybe society has finally accepted their existence.

    He turns to the shard of brick hearth from the remains of the Llano del Rio community and gets lost in its form. It's now the centerpiece of the lush floral growth some twenty feet toward the middle of the camp. The greenery surrounding it comprises a new habitat, so unlike the barren high desert where this utopian community thrived a century earlier, failing to a great extent because of water shortages. We want to continue that experiment, show that something vital can surface from its ashes and ruins. But this once real and functional memento is now more like an abstract piece of sculpture. Perhaps it reflects our desire to start over and avoid the mistakes of past experiments. If we let the ruins and the ashes be blown away by the force of time we might find ourselves living out scenarios that have little basis in achievable reality. After all, there seem to be limited options for crafting potentially perfect societies. And understandably, since utopia is an idea about a place that doesn't yet exist. It represents an asymptotic quest, a goal whose target lies well beyond the horizon. Each progressive advance pushes the horizon further. Some say it can never be realized—views vary throughout the group. But won't holding to this belief guarantee that no progress will be made?

He recalls the woman outside the fence and turns sharply in her direction. She's moved closer. He sees now that she has orange hair and thinks he recognizes her. Has she been observing him all this time? She suddenly throws her head back and laughs before scampering out of site. He dashes through the fence to get a better view, but she seems to have vanished into thin air. From this new vantage he spies a small crowd forming on the adjacent street and two black-and-whites cruising by in the distance. Reassured, he turns back inside.

He waves at Angela and Art who are admiring the mural on C Building with other residents. This is one of several that wrap the structures on the grounds with stories of their early struggles, the prior conditions of the city, and their link historically to other experiments. Beethoven's *Ninth Symphony* breezes through the crowd, its emotional nodes exposed in counterpoint to the moments of relative calm in the rhythmic effusions of chatter and merriment. Pumped by the sounds he hustles in their direction, going several feet beyond the sculpture and past the café to the amphitheater where people are beginning to gather for speeches and testimonials. It's a rough replica of the many theaters carved out of the hills and mountains of ancient Greece, but on a much smaller scale. A work of art in itself with excellent acoustics, it took several months to complete and is one of their proudest accomplishments.

"Come with us to the play, Todd!" shrieks Rhiannon, who materializes from his left, ushering a swarm of effervescing bodies. "It starts in a few minutes."

"I'm coming, you lovely people," he intones, reciprocating the invite by giving her and a few of the others big hugs. The play will be performed on the stage they constructed on the other side of the camp. Then he spots someone he doesn't recognize moving through the café. The sudden shift in the music to "God Bless America" scrambles his attention and the figure disappears.

"See someone over there?" asks Rhiannon.

"No... no one I... thought I did but I'll be over in a bit." The song transitions from one artist to another, the interpretations ranging from canned to free-form to satire and culminating with snippets from Madura's "Free From the Devil." The change in tone seems to recast the facial expressions of those in the swarm and others in the vicinity. This propels him through the crowd and into the café area where he's absorbed into the maelstrom.

The stage is nearly ready. A few hundred eager customers gather around the makeshift structure to witness their homegrown, indigenous creation. It's a one-act piece of improv that will repeat over the course of the day with a revolving cast of characters. The general theme is giving, thanks to the producers of this successful experiment consisting of all of those at the camp who in some way pitched in over the course of the year. In other words, they're dramatizing their creative roles and making offerings of themselves.

The amphitheater is full and the audience awaits the speakers. The first one is a Mr. Bohannon, the mayor's representative and city council member for the area, which encompasses the city. He's introduced by Ray.

"First let me say that the mayor apologizes for not being here in person for this special event. He had a previous engagement he wasn't able to cancel.

But believe me, he's extremely pleased at your success over the past year and proud to have your little city, if I may call it that, included in ours."

Claps sputter forth in sections but the overall effect is muted. The members look at each other as if they're not sure how to respond. His body language says he's not sure either. He pulls some notes from a folder and shuffles them anxiously, apparently trying to put them in the right order. More people from outside begin to gather not far from the fence. "The... all of you are to be commended for your... how you've helped to improve this part of the city. There are hardly any... transients... on the streets any longer. Your camp has found a way to nearly solve the city's homeless problem." The claps become more vigorous and sustained. The members, a good number of whom were formerly on the streets, glance at each other with congratulatory but skeptical nods. "We hope to keep working with you in..."

"All's going off according to plan so far," says Art, pulling Todd's attention away from the speech as he stands listening on the fringe. "Would've been nice to get the main man here, though. Bohannon, I'm not so sure about. He was only recently elected and... comes out of condo development. His company was responsible for a lot of the homelessness in town."

"Maybe he's been converted. Different culture down at city hall and... but frankly, I'd be shocked if anyone was much different. That's the system. That's why we put together our indie republic so we wouldn't have to compromise."

"I wonder if we can ever be entirely free of the system's influence." To this comment Todd can only look away from his imploring glance, and as he does he sees the woman with the orange hair again. She's sitting near the rear of the amphitheater and turns to meet his gaze, almost as if she expects him to single her out. She gets up and leaves the theater area on the side nearest the fence and then looks back his way and suddenly starts to twitch.

"That woman... she's... familiar but I haven't seen her here before," says Art. She walks slowly toward the speaker's platform, catching a glance from Mr. Bohannon as she passes by, and turns back again like she might want them to follow her. She continues walking along the fence and disappears. Did she leave the grounds, Todd wonders, or did she swing around behind B Building?

"Should we follow her?"

"Nah... we agreed to let outsiders in... she's probably a tourist, or maybe a friend of someone here. We don't want to exclude anyone."

"Maybe she's someone you met back before the camp existed. She looks familiar to me, too, but I can't place her. Odd mannerisms... maybe she's a casualty of Krassly's substance. I'll wander around and see if I can corner her."

As a number of citizens who were formerly denizens of the streets take their turns at the podium, testifying to their transformations, Todd cruises through the crowd and into the overflowing café area where Angela, Yram, and Cosmo are engaged in an intense conversation with Krassly at one of the tables.

"There's the man who made it all possible, put us over the edge... expanded our minds and... gave us a pretty good boost to our bodies too." Todd gives the substance guru a high-five.

The space in each of the buildings is reserved for displaying the fruits of the community's institutions—

the political, economic, social, and cultural offerings that it's flaunting to the world as evidence of the experiment they've advanced. This is what we are, they suggest to the public. Please bear witness to it. No preaching necessary.

Food production, for example. Though they still import a considerable amount of their food, more and more of their needs are being served through their organic garden, which occupies almost the entire space between the fence and C Building. The café is adjacent to the west end of this structure where the cafeteria is located, and a sumptuous spread of their healthy cuisine is now displayed. Hundreds have passed through here already.

Both A and B Building display the crafts that the community sells to help finance its operations—woven rugs, pottery, clothing, metalwork, jewelry, textiles, furniture, books, etc. They pride themselves on making items that are far superior in quality to those produced in the factory system. B Building is reserved for exhibiting their artwork, which is also for sale. Several members over the course of the year, most of whom were once homeless, have developed into notable artists whose works have been shown at galleries in the area. They've spawned a distinctive brand, what a critic at the monthly free paper called a refreshing alternative to the crass agitation and quasi-propaganda that socialist collectives often produce. It expresses points-of-view from the streets and the underside of society in an open, nonsectarian fashion. In the free space inside the buildings are workshops, open to the public, on political involvement, socializing, conversion therapy, etc. An assembly is planned at the end of the festivities to discuss the future. At the moment, these sites are flush with activity.

The woman with the orange hair wanders away from a group that's enjoying these fruits and continues strolling along the perimeter toward the shack at the far corner near A Building, which serves as the camp's physical plant. She brushes by the entrance, circles the structure, and peeks through one of its two windows before swinging back around to the entrance and tapping twice on the door. When nobody answers, she shuffles to the stage area.

How do these people survive with... they need an upgrade, the male inside the shack reflects. This place is like their minds, their groupie heads. These wires... they don't seem to go anywhere... like them, they're a bunch of frayed ends that need to be clipped and smoothed over... loose ends that need to be connected and reconnected. Here we are, just have to splice a few of the right ones together or... the wrong ones and... well...

Power is their problem. They need to use it more efficiently and for different purposes... make themselves stronger and stop trying to help the weak who don't deserve it. That'll do it. He hears two taps on the door and after a few minutes peeks through the slit, steps out, and bolts to the carnival.

The play that's starting is a variation on one of the chosen themes for the festivities: Renewal and Reinvention. It's not a play, a staged dramatic action, in the usual sense. At the moment the stage is being cleared of the players who acted in the previous performance, and Heather appears to explain what's next. She asks for volunteers from the audience to come up and help them put this one together, which elicits giggles from a few sectors and a stirring of interest in others. These exchange skeptical glances as if they're asking their mate or acquaintance or neighbor: "Can I really go up there and act? Is it possible?" They seem to get confirmation from sizing each other up, like one person's look is a mirror that reflects encouraging data back to another.

"We need several of you who are open to searching for a role that will coincide with the character you want to mature through... and especially the one that will allow you to begin reinventing yourself for the purpose of striving toward perfection."

Snickers and guffaws from itinerant disbelievers are succeeded by robust applause from the choir, which spreads and brings a dribble of aspiring dramatists to the stage.

"Just a few more and we're set," Heather says, clearly pleased with the response. Several now stream toward the stage but she cuts if off at two. Once all the recruits are gathered she signals offstage and some vets join them, rounding off the group into ten members including herself—four males and six females. The audience gawks, wishing to suspend its disbelief for a little longer, and Heather says, "Okay, let's huddle!"

The novices appear stupefied but the vets gather them into a circle of nervous limbs that settle into a blob of spurting interchanges, then into what resembles an organic growth of whispering dialogues. It remains like this for a few minutes and the audience, noticeably entertained, is ready for the punch line. But the growth doesn't separate; it appears to congeal even more. Several more minutes elapse and members of the audience begin to exchange stares with each other, growing edgy. A few sardonic catcalls erupt, along with expressions that beg for consummation.

Smiles surface from a few others like they seem to know what they're discussing inside the bubble.

Todd—who has been taking it all in from the rear as he tries to keep an eye out for the woman with orange hair—is one of these and wishes he could be a fly buzzing around Heather's face. The elapsed time approaches ten minutes and the frustration mounts further. A few in the audience get up and leave, vanishing through the fence into the other city. How much longer will they stretch our patience, Todd wonders, though he appreciates this adventure in consciousness-raising. How much longer before everyone either walks out or rushes the stage?

A male behind Todd begins to laugh. It starts out as a choppy, guttural squirt like he's trying to hold the pleasure back but is having a difficult time doing so until its weaker forms sputter forth through the audience and he lets it go. Then it breaks into an orgasmic gush of giddiness that seems to feed on itself, like when the awareness of laughter's excess becomes a contagion in the laugher's own mind and the reason for it disappears into a total abandonment to its effects. This releases the tension and snickers compound throughout the audience which breaks out in self-congratulatory applause, not unlike motorists in an epic gridlock on a rush-hour freeway who one minute fantasize taking out their anger on their fellow prisoners and the next are partying with them in the back of a van. He bolts up to the stage, his arrival a signal that un-fuses the group, which he now joins.

Todd now recognizes the plant as Cosmo, though he's disguised. The members onstage turn to the audience and smile exuberantly, like they've been transformed inside the bubble into a tight-knit family. Todd wonders if they've taken Krassly's substance.

"We want to start by offering a short meditation to those souls who've been lost to the outer city's barbarous policies," Heather says as she drops cross-legged to the stage floor, followed by the others. "They've led to foreclosures, the theft of property, and the disruption of so many lives. Our community is pledged to preventing that from happening again."

The meditation continues for another minute until one member of the group snaps out of it, and then the rest in a choppy chain reaction. Most of the audience simulates the same maneuver and once its collective attention is grooved on the stage Heather passes the baton to Prunella, who introduces "the play."

"I've been thinking about the issues we discussed in our huddles for a long time and I'm excited that I can talk about them because I've admired what this camp has done all along. I live close by and have been in the city for a long time and seen many problems and I always wondered why so many people are treated badly. If each of us became a better person this wouldn't happen anymore. We lose touch with who we are and we need to look at ourselves once in a while so we can be our best. I want to be a person who gives more time to others... pays more attention to those who get ignored and become victims of bad people. That's the character I want to perform in our drama."

She peruses the group with a zesty smile that lingers as the applause from the audience increases and she's beaming with the confident grin of someone who has just successfully completed her first audition.

Todd continues to scope the area from the rear while taking in this preface to the play. What a refreshing addition Prunella would make to the community, he reflects, with her passion and... a voice that gets you to listen, a presence that says she's not acting. But these are the skills you need to act. He remembers a few of his early auditions, especially one for a play at a downtown experimental theater and how the experience made him more reflective. You can't act well without knowing what it means to behave truthfully and honestly and believe in something. Reinvention is acting, trying out roles that make sense for who you are at the moment. And you can't reinvent yourself unless you have a firm self-concept to start with. He now understands how the community can influence people to become themselves. He thinks he spots the woman with orange hair in the crowd on the fringe of the café and drifts a few feet into the crowd for a better look.

"I agree with her," segues Jalen, hitching on the vibes from Prunella's performance. "I've been here for five months and I... can't stop changing. The people and the stuff we do here make me wanna try to do different things and... I do them and... it's like we're in a play all the time... take new vows almost every day to be better and set new goals for ourselves. I feel like I know so much more about myself now. If we could try out all kinds of roles with each other and learn what they mean we could be a great society. We make our society. We don't need anyone else to do it for us. If we don't keep at it we'll... die! I wanna play the character of one of those people that are after us and try to figure out what they want... what they get out of doing bad things to us. How did they get like that? I wanna learn that and get ready for what we need to do in the future and..."

The audience hushes, expecting his trail of ideas to stretch on. And the expression on his face suggests he wants to accommodate them. But as he gazes with apprehension into the ether between their faces he lets out a deep breath of closure that suspends the hush for a few more seconds until it breathes applause into the space and into his mind, pumping him with confidence.

He passes through the entrance and into the queue at the checkout desk of the library feeling somewhat skittish since he has never spent much time in this public sanctuary. The last time was a couple years ago when he had to do some research on a client. Not much seems to have changed. He doesn't see anyone who's reading books or other material. The computers are all being used, probably by the usual losers checking out the porn sites. Why do we even need libraries anymore? The woman in front of him looks around, starts screaming, and bolts out the door. He steps to the counter.

"Can I help you?" a buoyant punkish princess with horn-rimmed glasses asks.

"I... need to talk to Mr. Osgood about... settling some back fines."

"He's in the back... I'll get him," she snips while pivoting away, then turns back for a second look while he's scoping the entrance. Mr. Osgood hustles his corpulent frame to the counter a few minutes later like a good civil servant and stares at him like he's expecting him to say something, but he merely pleads for direction with his eyes while trying to place him.

"Come on back," says Mr. Osgood as he opens the swinging half door, looking around the space as he addresses him.

"You can't bring that backpack into this area," spouts the punkish princess, her interest in him revived.

"It's okay," returns Mr. Osgood. "I can vouch for him. This won't take long."

He follows Mr. Osgood into the back and he directs him through a door in the corner and to an iron spiral staircase, making sure she's not looking. "It'll take you to the roof. When you come back down you can exit there." He takes a couple steps to his right and points to a door with a "no exit" sign. "I've disabled the alarm."

He nods in appreciation and makes his way to the top, exiting onto a bulging surface of neglect. He sidesteps a few swells on his way to the waist-high wall around the edge, but his left foot manages to alight on a soft spot and it dips a few inches, nearly upending him. Reaching the wall he gazes off into the distance, first at the sea, and then at the streets below. They were right, he reflects. This is the perfect vantage. And the day is so clear, with barely any crosswinds.

He deposits his backpack next to the wall and scans this tarred wasteland of protruding cubes. Near the center of the roof there's a large rectangular box that looks like it could be the entrance to another stairway. There are no high rises in the immediate area but he stays down and belly-crawls to the structure. The door is on the other side and he checks it, satisfying himself that it's locked, and returns to the wall. He then opens his backpack and examines the contents.

Todd keeps the woman in his sights as he slips into the crowd but she vanishes into a cluster of scattering bodies. Thinking she'll reappear he picks up the pace, plunging into the heart of the café. But she's nowhere to be seen. He sees Rhiannon with a group at a nearby table and she waves him over.

"You seem so... serious," she says as he plops down on a chair to join them. "Aren't you having fun?"

"No... no... nothing like that. I saw this woman... she's been floating around and I want to find out who it is. She has orange hair. Have you seen her?"

"I probably have but it's a colorful day and... every imaginable hue on the most amazing rainbow is..."

"...you got into Krassly's..."

He sees a flash of orange appear around the side of the adjacent building and rises slowly from his chair, feeling that if he moves too fast she might vanish again. Shuffling into the crowd that separates them he sees her more clearly and shields himself behind a cluster of animated revelers. He still doesn't recognize her. It seems like she's miming something to someone off to her right, making a special effort to gesticulate properly to compensate for the tumult. She abruptly veers to her left into his field of vision and now seems to be channeling someone else. He slips behind another barrier of bodies for a protected perspective and tries to identify who she's communicating with, but with no success. She flits off as he peruses the crowd.

"I agree... the best way to prepare for the future is to find out why these enemies have to force us to be a certain way. I wanna play the character of a mind polluter... a holy person who talks from a distance to anonymous people through words in books, scriptures that screen us from the truth... and are always against the body." Oros reaches behind her and grabs a stack of books, placing them on stage in front of her. "Jesus, Muhammad, Friedman... they all say the same kinds of things." She begins to shred the pages of all the books and toss the paper shards into the air. They float toward the crowd and the capricious breeze-currents carry them in various directions. A few aeronautical accidents stream to the edge of the crowd and alight like mutant snowflakes on people's laps.

"You can't... you can't do that to those... those are sacred books and you'll..." The heckler, a lanky, energized man of about thirty rushes the stage waving what appears to be a pocket Bible. Before he can finish his sentence, Oros strips, freezing him in his tracks. She tosses her clothes to a group rapt to her provocative lesson, and they brace themselves for the next prong in the plot. The lucky targets pluck pieces from the air and press them to their breasts like they're talismans transferring her mindset to them. Then *they* start to strip. This spreads to others in the audience and boomerangs back to the other nine.

He peers over the edge at the festivities down and across the way, caressing his precision instrument, its cold steel heating up in his hands that now begin to sweat, the moisture oozing through his body like steam through an engine. His body stiffens but his heart is palpitating and he backs a few feet away from the wall to take several deep, undulant breaths, then inches back into position. Now composed, he looks through the scope at the clear and crisp faces and smiles. No mess-ups this time. He can't miss. His field of vision is as transparent as his conscience. This assignment will let him prove himself, cancel that lapse from a year ago, and renew his purpose in life as a soldier for justice.

Where is she? She's supposed to direct him. Why are all those people on the other side of that building? No cops. Perfect! What... what's that woman doing? Something isn't right. Where is she? I don't see anyone I remember. I can't identify anyone. What? Is this some big strip show or something? Why do people always have to expose themselves in public? These are definitely amateurs. Not much silicone. Where's that woman? She said she'd be wearing orange. There she is! A sound breaks his concentration. He turns to see the door opening behind him and two masked figures dressed in dark baggy clothes emerge, keeping a tight grip on his instrument as he tries to process the interruption. He suspects there must've been a change of plans.

"Don't think I need any help... fellas. Who... sent you?"

They don't respond, but inch toward him while separating, making it difficult to form an impression of either. One is of medium height and stocky, the other taller and wiry.

"Why the masks?"

"Our work is always... hush-hush, as you know," says the stocky one.

"Do I know you? Your voice sounds familiar." They continue to slip further apart as they come closer.

"We've come to relieve you of your command, soldier," says the wiry one as they stop on opposite sides of him.

"Relieve me of... what're you talking about?" He clutches his instrument. In the ensuing silence he eyes the wiry one and then the stocky one, fixing on what little of the latter's face he can spy in an effort to identify him. In the space of this brief diversion the wiry one springs at him like a rattlesnake, grabbing his neck before he can maneuver out of the way, and applying the pressure that renders a person unconscious.

"How much time we got?" asks the stocky one as they drag him out of the way.

"Perty much on time," says the other as they proceed to assemble their weapons. "This is a mighty fine piece a work. Too bad he won't get ta use it."

"Do they want us to get rid of the woman too?"

"Yeah, if we have time and can pull it off. But it's not the highest priority."

The stripping-chain snakes through the audience, drawing copycats and a few of the timid into a whirlwind of physical sensations that encourage them to brandish their bodies through the growing piles of clothes and open up to their neighbors. And suddenly they're writing themselves into the drama, contemplating roles of their own and testing them out. Some are adversely provoked and want the naturalists to put their clothes back on. A few from this group become quite strident and proceed to reunite the errant coverings with their proper owners, playing pin the panties and bras on the babes—jockeys on the dudes. As the redressing factions get more vocal a contingent of sympathizers filters in from outside the perimeter, a few waving what appear to be Bibles while the players on stage descend into the audience.

In the chaos, the woman with orange hair surfaces on the opposite side of the stage area from where Todd is still perusing the crowd. She seems flustered, like she's lost someone, and glances up at the top of the library, stares intently for several seconds, then steps closer to the clothing melee. More bodies strip and more from outside stream onto the grounds, and the increasing scale of the activity forces

Art, Yram, Ray, and Krassly from their locations. The woman with orange hair studies the changing dynamics and again looks up at the top of the library, then points her finger at this convening group. After waiting for several seconds, she saunters over and brushes by Art, Ray, and Yram, glancing once again at the top of the library before nodding at each one. Meanwhile, Todd observes her actions and hustles in her direction as an explosion occurs in the rear of the grounds, nixing the lights and the music. As most everyone's attention cranes toward the sound, the woman's expression pulses with satisfaction. But Todd only fleetingly acknowledges the explosion, continuing his trek toward her and catching some very familiar mannerisms as he arrives in her presence.

"It's you!" he exclaims. "Why are you here? What's with the cheesy getup?"

She delivers a clownish, gotcha smile and pivots into view, staring for the requisite moment to the top of the library, piquing Todd's interest. She pivots back with a satisfied smirk.

"Looking for new areas to clean up and improve? Or do you want to join the free spirits?"

Shots ring out and everyone scatters through the screaming din toward cover or the exits. Todd looks directly up where she looked and lurches rapidly to his left as a bullet grazes his shoulder, striking a tall blond seraphic spirit dressed in a dangling bandana. He drops to the ground and crawls behind a few overturned chairs, hailing Rhiannon as she obliviously sprints by, and hustles to the fringe of the fray behind a bulky cactus to survey the mayhem. Art lies motionless on the ground and a writhing Yram is spread across two chairs. Todd sputter-steps toward her but falls back as he notices two unfamiliar, overdeveloped muscle mannequins commandeering a guardian while several more private security types move warily among the remaining customers, brandishing small weapons. Several of the players, including Oros and Heather and some sympathizers in the audience remain around the stage. They appear to be in a state of shock and refuse to move, like staying planted in the same spot on this special ground might keep the memory of this space alive a little longer. Suddenly a ragtag film crew rushes by and converges in front of the stage, getting as much footage of the scene as possible, especially the naked bodies and the piles of clothing strewn around it. A woman, who appears to be the director of the crew, infiltrates the awestruck naturalists.

"Who's in charge here? Don't look. act natural. Don't look at the camera!"

"Where's the cops?" a fully dressed, burly male hollers as he hobbles by.

"I make movies," continues the woman while peering over her shoulder at the people, especially the gun-wielders. Sirens scream in the distance. "My name is Amy."

Oros stares at her in disbelief, giving her the impression that she's the one to speak to, but remains speechless. She offers Amy her limp hand and she clasps it with both of hers.

"We don't have much time. Here's my card. I live in a loft in an abandoned church on Venice Way. We're making an XXX art film in that space with piles of Bibles and many different denominational bodies getting spiritual. We've got the contracts ready to be signed."

Before Oros or anyone else can respond, the crew vanishes toward the rear. Todd wants to join them to find out what they were talking about but the sirens are getting closer. He decides to follow the crew's lead when he feels the ground rumbling, like it might be the start of an earthquake. He looks to his right as a monster dozer passes heedless through the opening in the fence, followed by another and another and... He vaults to his left for cover behind a clump of bushes and watches them passing by to the accompaniment of the piercing sirens. On the side of each machine in big letters are the words "Hyperion Improvement Group." They clamor off in different directions, like each has been programmed to search for and destroy specific targets, evading the sectors of activity where bodies are being cared for, revving through gears toward a threshold of fear, the decibel variations in each coiling into a dissonant ditty of RPM aggression.

"What're you doing here?" a spry and lean fifties-something woman wearing granny glasses asseverates after a dozer passes through the stage area like a tank through an outhouse. "What've we done? Where's the help... the cops?" She leaps onto the dozer's shovel fisting the anonymous driver in defiance, but a security guard-type hustles over and pulls her out, depositing her on a heap of rubble.

The machines continue on their foreordained paths, industry-molded masses crunching and flattening anything natural or crafted through the serendipity of human invention, paring back idiosyncrasy to the identical and manageable, the functional and utilitarian. Todd sees one of these prehistoric techno-predators roll over the Llano del Rio sculpture in the far corner, spewing its pieces in all different directions like gravel. Another plows through the café area and stops, a primeval mind pondering its prey. The sirens reach the exit and several officers appear, followed by a team of paramedics. They glide onto the grounds like they're moving through a different dimension. The officers peer around the grounds befuddled, not sure what they're supposed to be doing, and are soon met by several of the security guard-types. They then fan out toward the dozers as if they now understand their role. The paramedics pile the bodies onto stretchers and hustle them off the grounds.

    Todd cranes to see what condition they're in, but the dust stirred up by the machines screens him from a clear look. The brownish fog gets denser and he nearly chokes, but after several inhales his senses seem transformed. It's the smell that first captures him, not the nose-twitching mustiness that's mostly neutral, a slight encumbrance, something to be eliminated through the march of progress as decay, waste, transition, the intimation of death, but a nose-sucking nectar that draws him in, perks him up to life. Can dust speak, deliver answers to latent questions? It's like the dust stirring from all over the camp somehow attaches to different sectors, sub-pockets and enclaves of extraordinarily intense experiments in living where the vibes and juices and smells are still potent and powerful and their stewing together produces the equivalent of an ambrosial substance. He breathes it in for several seconds, letting it suffuse through his body, and smiles, fighting off the urge to burst out laughing. Did someone cook a gourmet batch of nitrous oxide and spray it over the area to zap the survivors? Or is this a self-induced mechanism of escape from the horror around him?

    The dozer-grinding seems choppier and multi-sonorous. He hears snips of distorted, overlapping conversations but no one seems close to him. Are spirits speaking to him? Those of the just departed? Others who feel violated by this invasion? Or are they only voices in his head? Dust clouds begin to form overhead and take on the rough outlines of familiar faces and some threatening ones before morphing into other, more enigmatic shapes. A large flock of pigeons passes over the area, several descending on the camp, alighting on the mounds of rubble. They remain stationary, gazing around like the effusion of chaos has spiked their perceptual abilities up the evolutionary chain. One, then another, and finally the rest zigzag toward the heavens but stop above the camp and hover, transforming into white doves. These start to circle and after a few laps swoop down as vultures.

ALTZ HOUSE

"How'd you hear about us, Mr. Bretoff ?" asks the sixtyish, silver-haired woman at the table.

"I... don't remember exactly. I think it was..."

"Mr. Bretoff... Mr. Bretoff... you okay?"

"I... sure... I was just thinking about... something." His tentative expression frames dilating eyes.

"How'd you hear about us?"

"From my... this woman over at the café on... she said she had this old boyfriend whose brother was here and..." He stops and gawks to the right where two males are painting the walls, then turns back with a mottled grin.

"Good... we love to get referrals from satisfied customers."

"And I... think my ex might... be here... or was here when..."

He gazes off to his left and lasers the movements of a woman racing down the hallway in a wheelchair, mumbling something to herself.

"What's her name?"

"Well, she used to go by... but she changed that when she went to... guess that was another friend who went into the convent and then..."

"Maybe you'll recognize her tomorrow when you come back. You can eat with us. Would you like that?"

"I'm... not sure if... I can but... if I can I would like..."

"Mr. Bretoff, you okay? Do you wanna lay down for a while? Can I get you a water?"

"No... no, no I think I need to leave."

"Something bothering you? You look like you've seen a ghost."

"Nothing that I... this place makes me feel like I've been here before and something bad happened."

"Here? We've only been here for a short while. I don't remember ever seeing you here. Are you sure you have the right place?"

"Oh... I don't know... I just feel... who was here before?"

"I don't know for sure... think it was a café some years ago, then a mission."

"Oh... really? I kinda re... member going to some places like that but then I'm not too sure... so..."

"...you're probably confusing this place with somewhere else."

"When I was a young... I think I used to come somewhere around here. Maybe the building that used to be here was..."

"Was what, Mr. Bretoff?"

"Maybe it *was* a café back..."

"Back when?"

"I can't remember for sure. I think it was when..."

"When, Mr. Bretoff?"

"When that guy was president who..."

"Who was that?"

"I... .don't know. Who was that... lady in the wheelchair?"

"That someone you remember from when we had this president?"

"I don't... she looks like someone who used to be at that club over on... the Rig or something and... but maybe that was somebody... else."

"Well, we'd love to have you be part of our family if it's the right place for you and if you... qualify. Can I get some information from you, Mr. Bretoff?"

"What do... you mean?"

"We wanna make sure you will feel at home here."

"At home?"

"We wanna make you feel like you're part of our community and will stay until... well, we don't wanna see you unhappy."

"Oh... okay."

"How do you feel about other people, Mr. Bretoff ? Are there any people you don't like being around?"

"Well... those people who're always making all that noise up by the Center who... but I think I like just about everyone else."

"What about girls... I mean women?"

"I like... to sit on the bench by the pagoda and peek at them as they go down to the water."

"Sure, that's only natural. But do you enjoy being around them and... interacting with them?"

"Inter... yeah, yeah... I like to... I ran into Sophie last month at the Center and we had a nice chat about..."

"About what?"

"About some of the good times we had when we..."

"Well, I'm sure you'll find some good companionship here, too, and maybe even renew some old acquaintances."

"I think I would... like that."

"Do you like to share with people and participate in activities, Mr. Bretoff?"

"I like to help other people and..."

"And what?"

"And... I like to get something back when I deserve it."

"That's... pretty normal. And do you like to join activities with people you don't know very well?"

"As long as... I like to do new things with some but..."

"But what?"

"But... not with..."

"Well, you think about that and we'll revisit it. What's your financial situation like?"

"I have a bank account at the... co-op over on..."

"Sure... the co-op. Do you have documentation of your net worth?"

"Net... worth?"

"Yes, like your recent tax returns?"

"I think I have that... it's over at..."

"Try to find that information and bring it to us as soon as you can. We don't accept applicants who are independently wealthy. We have a cap on income level and asset ownership. All of your needs will be taken care of here so you'll have no worries. You'll be relieved of the burden of having to manage your finances. You'll be free to pursue your dreams and goals... the values of an alternative lifestyle to perfection."

"I value..."

The building is one of the first constructed along the boardwalk, built in the first few years of the twentieth century as a hotel but since adapted to the sundry uses of various owners and occupiers. Abandoned quite recently and threatened with demolition, a consortium of concerned citizens purchased it and leased it to a group of artists, therapists, and pharmacologists. The consensus was to preserve and upgrade the fossil of the older structure while adding a modern facade with lots of windows for light and a view of the ocean. Workers are currently putting the finishing touches on it. Just to the right of the entrance is a large, discolored wooden arch hewn with indentations and markings and positioned in a small garden of succulents. Several folks are currently milling around it.

"What do you think this is?" asks a woman with a long gray ponytail, admiring the arch like it's a work of art on display at the Los Angeles Louvre.

"Oh, maybe it's... your guess is as good as mine," returns a portly male with a cane. He's squinting to bring the image into clearer focus.

"Who knows," blurts a genderless voice from the fringe. "But where did they get it and... why did they put it here?"

A woman with a frizzed-out, reddish-gray Afro sashays through the tangle to the arch, disrupting the momentary stupor. She looks it over, takes a deep breath, and walks circumspectly through it, turning slowly to face the leering crowd before strutting back.

"It makes me feel... like I've been on a trip into... the future and back," she says, giggling to the gallery.

"Or... into the past and... returning to..." The portly male mouths a few latent syllables.

"Returning to what?" asks another gray ponytail with granny glasses as she creeps up behind him and massages his midsection. He stumbles into the woman next to him, who's tall and very thin, her baggy clothes obscuring what was likely a model's body. He manages a vacant smirk.

"To bed!" rips an anonymous voice. "I need a nap." A concordance of chuckles suffuses the crowd as it disperses toward the front door of the building and files inside.

The giddy mood presses into the lobby, sparking surprised looks from those schmoozing at a few tables. The entrants spread around and begin to mingle, the mood now modulating. A few languish alone on the sofas and gawk at the spectacle. A florid, loquacious Q-tip jerks up from a table and waddles to a sofa, bending over directly in front of a man who's staring off to the right. She turns and sees the apparent object of his vision, a rusty-haired sixtyish woman busting out of a string bikini.

"Do you know her?" she asks, unable to break his trance. "That's Lisa... she used to be a stripper over at the... somewhere on... Washington, I think. She still likes to show off her silicone. Are you the new arrival? I'm Clara."

"New arrival?" He turns to face her.

"You just got here?"

"Yeah, that's... right. I just got here... a while ago. I'm... Andre. Andre. I..."

"Yes... you what?" He jerks his attention toward the string bikini and lasers her, though she doesn't return it. He shuffles away and alights on another sofa across the room, crosses his legs, and gazes at the wall.

"Charming the new male residents again, Clara!" exhorts a lanky woman wearing a slightly oversized tie-dyed tee who's been tracking the trajectories. She rises and saunters over to the sofa, sporting a quizzical smile. Clara remains on the periphery, bemused.

"I'm Jane," offers the tie-dyed tee, edging her body onto the sofa. She has an unflinching smile that exudes life-and-people-are-beautiful but giggles periodically. At the very edge of each eruption her expression becomes vacant, like a subliminal flash threatens to dissolve her upbeat mood before she returns to form.

"You must be our new member," she continues, "the one everybody's been talkin' about."

He's in the process of forming a syllable when Lisa plops down on the other side of the sofa, quashing his verbal efforts and re-engaging his gaze. He appears deep in thought.

"Not much to talk about because..."

"Why, Andre?" asks Jane, drawing his gaze halfway toward her.

"I haven't talked to anybody about much... yet and..."

"And?" He now turns toward her while still keeping an eye on Lisa, who's seemingly oblivious to their conversation.

"And I haven't had a... chance."

"Maybe your reputation precedes you. Have you lived around here?"

"Yeah, I used to live down..."

"Down?"

"Down... somewhere around the... guess maybe that was a long... time ago."

"How long?" Before Jane can finish he jerks up and arcs to about five feet in front of Lisa and stops quickly, like he's decided not to address her. He observes her intently for several seconds until she slowly makes eye contact, then gracefully angles away toward Jane, who notices and looks at him quizzically.

After locking on her gape like he's come under a spell, he turns back to Lisa and fixes on her necklace.

Curious, Jane rises and joins his sightline. "Hey, what's so fascinating about Lisa's neck?" Lisa looks at Jane as if to second the question and then directly at Andre, who's now squinting as he inspects the area below her necklace, a swatch of crepy freckles that points like an arrow to the deep valley cleaving her fleshy masses. Lisa reaches behind her back and undoes the strap of her bikini top, causing it to slip down slightly. Her eyes are like flames combusting from smoldering ashes.

"Lisa, what's got into you?" interjects Jane.

Andre, meanwhile, continues to inspect the new terrain, his penetrating gaze seeming to firm up her skin which now reveals a shapely mole.

Jane steps to the right of Lisa and stretches onto the sofa, reaching behind to fasten her strap. Andre's gaze remains fixed on the mole like he's mesmerized by the afterimage of a flashing neon sign.

An electronic, genderless voice reverberates from the ceiling.

"Attention everyone... attention! We're gathering in the auditorium for our five minutes of peace and love at the top of the hour. Please don't be late."

The sound seems to secrete an invisible chemical into the room and everyone slows down as expressions become pensive but expectant. They fall into single file and march methodically through the door. Andre scans the ephemera pulsing from the wall...

The room is spacious and brightly lit, the walls patterned with random paintings, posters, and portraits. The chairs are full of residents whose attention is focused on the screen in front where images are beginning to flicker in tandem with soft music as the lights dim. Faint lyrics surface and gradually become more distinct as an instrumental arrangement of "White Bird" transitions into an eclectic mashup. A field of daisies fills the screen, the camera zooming in to afford a glimpse of what appear to be clusters of bodies contorting through the petals before it pulls back. It repeats, but each time it does the camera offers a slightly different vantage of the bodies. The lyrics of "White Bird" press through the sounds as naked limbs entwine with the flowers, fading to a spike of instrumental riffs that are quickly layered with the electronic voice, this time inflected an octave higher.

"Now hug each other... move around the room and spread love to your brothers and sisters."

The riffs keep repeating as some pivot eagerly to mostly willing targets while others inch timidly toward moving shapes and flail for hugs. Many find vacant spaces but continue the search. Meanwhile, the body parts on the screen evolve into Frisbees floating off in various directions, each transforming into one, then another human shape before converting back to an inanimate plastic disk. It conjures a hiccupping organism.

A scream surges through the room as the lights flash on and off.

"Attention everyone... attention!" peals the electronic voice with a trace of urgency. "Please be careful... respect your neighbor!"

The interruption snuffs the scream, leaving a stretch of silence that seems to alter the cadence of the flashing lights. Snickers and then a few giggles puncture the void as the lights stabilize, slightly brighter than before. This allows most to see others around them more clearly and the configuration of exploratory hugging changes. The riffs return as the Frisbees on the screen morph into peace signs, the observing countenances registering various degrees of blissful resignation.

"That's it... that's it!" peals the voice. "But move around, spread your love... reach out and touch someone!"

The scene resembles a Chinese fire drill, the urgency dissipating with each movement. Some touch while others graze toward their nominal target without quite reaching it and slumber off toward another choice. The riffs slow and distort, then abruptly terminate as the lights brighten fully and the voice rises.

"Time's up... time's up! Return to your rooms and savor the good feelings you've received today and... rest up for our activities later. There'll be a poetry reading in the library... a group therapy session in the conference room... a seminar on libido retrieval here... an anger management class in..."

"...ehhhhhhhh... haaaahhhhh... no, no!" screams a tall, wispy but spry Q-tip in the rear with long, stringy hair swaying from her efforts to get away from a frenzy of groping hands. All eyes turn toward the action as the woman evades their reach and slips to the exit.

"I told you last week I don't remember ever meeting you," she says, inching through the doorway.

The male pursuer continues searching as if he's comfortable flailing at her physical echo, slow in processing her words or perhaps just hard of hearing.

"What do you mean?" asks the handsome, burly hulk with a sagging paunch whose instinctual energies seem to be in the process of dissembling. He turns sharply around, the Q-tip now nearly out the door. "You said the other day you wanted to be..."

"...be what? You got the wrong person... I've

never talked to you."

Several genderless figures wearing white coats rush through the doorway. One grabs the male's arms and takes him from the room. He goes willingly but with a puzzled expression on his face. The other white coats meander through the skittish crowd.

The first scream proves to be contagious—a second erupts from the other side of the room and the white coats skip to the source, then another spikes from an unknown location before the first stops, the overlay delivering a sonorous screech. A small crowd gathers near the center of the room and the white coats surround them.

"Don't touch me... get away from me!" screams a woman gyrating at the center of a crowd, her short, brownish-orange hair seeming to frizz out in rhythm to her movement. She swivels a choppy, incomplete three-sixty, gazing at the rapt expressions, then stops suddenly as if on stage and delivers an apologetic curtsy. As she faces the group again, her matronly mien dissolves and her countenance pulses with confidence.

"Why are all of you looking at... me... like that?" she asks while stepping to the edge of the crowd, forging a path through the awestruck bodies to the waiting clasps of white coats on the other side. As they escort her from the room a male jettisons from the group and impales himself against the wall, arms spread parallel to the floor. Occupied with his own mental imagery, he's oblivious to the gallery's stares.

"Relax, everyone... relax. Please return to your rooms."

Most trudge anxiously through the door while a few stragglers ogle the male, who remains frozen against the wall as the white coats beeline their way to him.

Andre is wedged into the corner of the room in squat formation like he's ready to spring up at any moment. Lisa returns his gaze from a few feet away as she slowly angles to the exit. They become locked in addled trances, freezing Lisa's momentum and straining Andre's expression. This brief meeting of minds seems to secrete a chemical that awakens his memory. As the strain dissipates, he becomes energized with a new confidence and clarity.

"Lisa... Lisa!" he exhorts, springing in her direction. "It was in that spacious upper-level living room at that mansion on the boardwalk, just down from the Lafayette." He's now facing her. She's still ready to make her escape but is now curious.

"Remember?" he asks.

Her expression contorts as he continues. "All the windows were open. There was lots of natural light streaming in. Sensual music was coming from speakers on the ceiling. It was late afternoon, the Fourth of July, 1979." She seems pleasantly puzzled, her eyes flickering with recognition.

"The beautiful screams from so many throats," he adds. "The odor of sweat and pungent lilacs."

Lisa curls her lips ever so slightly and flashes a caustic smile while slowly stepping away from him. Then suddenly, she turns around, fixes on him for several seconds, and screams in a cascade of high pitch variances. Two white coats appear and gently guide her out. Though there's terror in her eyes, she continues to look at him as she backs through the exit. Andre rushes after her.

"What are you doing on Saturday night?"

John O'Kane has published over two hundred essays, op-eds, stories and articles as well as four books: *Venice, CA: A City State of Mind; A People's Manifesto*; *Jukebox Confessionals; and Toward Election 2020: Cancel Culture, Censorship and Class*. He also publishes and edits *AMASS* Magazine and teaches writing at the University of California.

Dan Marcus is a playwright, screenwriter, songwriter, and managing editor of AMASS magazine.

Thank you to the Wapshott Press sponsors, supporters, and Friends of the Wapshott Press.

Muna Deriane
Kit Ramage
Rachel Livingston
Ann and John Brantingham
David Meischen
Thomas Loper
Laurel Sutton
John O'Kane
Suzanne Siegel
Toni Rodriguez
James and Rebecca White
Ronni Kern
Steve Misuraca
Robert Earle and Mary Azoy
LindaAnn LoSchivao
James Wilson
Kathleen Warner
Alice Frances Wickham
Leslie Bohem
Phil Temples
Richard Whittaker

The Wapshott Press is a 501(c)(3) not-for-profit press publishing work by emerging and established authors and artists. We publish books that should be published. We are very grateful to the people who believe in our plans and goals, as well as our hopes and dreams. Our website is at www.WapshottPress.org. Donations gratefully accepted at www.Donate.WapshottPress.org.

Made in the USA
Columbia, SC
17 March 2022